Lina was about to say goodbye to Doon, but he took hold of her arm. "Lina," he said, "look at this." There was something in his voice that made her turn to him in surprise. He held out the book, pointing at smaller print at the cover's lower edge.

Lina peered at it. "For the people from Em," it said, and then there was a blot of something on the last part of the word. But it didn't matter. She knew what the word was. She looked up at Doon, wide-eyed.

"Ember," they said, both speaking at the same time.

Praise for the City of Ember Books

An American Library Association
Notable Children's Book

A *Kirkus Reviews* Editors' Choice

A New York Public Library
100 Titles for Reading and Sharing Selection

A *Child Magazine* Best Children's Book

A Mark Twain Award Winner

A William Allen White Children's Book
Award Winner

★ "Part mystery, part adventure story."
—*VOYA*, Starred

"A solid and satisfying conclusion."
—*School Library Journal*

"The conclusion is everything a series closer
should be, satisfying but provocative."
—*The Horn Book Magazine*

"Fast-paced and clever."
—*Kirkus Reviews*

Also by Jeanne DuPrau

The City of Ember

The People of Sparks

The Diamond of Darkhold

The Prophet of Yonwood

Voyagers: *Escape the Vortex*

THE CITY OF EMBER

BOOK 3

THE DIAMOND OF DARKHOLD

Jeanne DuPrau

A YEARLING BOOK

Text copyright © 2008 by Jeanne DuPrau
Cover art copyright © 2016 by Paul Sullivan and Bryan Lashelle
Logo art copyright © 2016 by Jacey
Map by Chris Riely

All rights reserved. Published in the United States by Yearling, an imprint of Random House
Children's Books, a division of Penguin Random House LLC, New York. Originally published in
hardcover in the United States by Random House Children's Books, New York, in 2008.

Yearling and the jumping horse design are registered trademarks
of Penguin Random House LLC.

Visit us on the Web! randomhousekids.com

Educators and librarians, for a variety of teaching tools,
visit us at RHTeachersLibrarians.com

The Library of Congress has cataloged the hardcover edition of this work as follows:
DuPrau, Jeanne.
The diamond of Darkhold / Jeanne DuPrau.
p. cm.
Summary: When a roamer trades them an ancient book with only a few pages remaining,
Lina and Doon return to Ember to seek the machine the book seems to describe in hopes
that it will get their new community, Sparks, through the winter.
ISBN 978-0-375-85571-9 (trade) — ISBN 978-0-375-95571-6 (lib. bdg.) —
ISBN 978-0-375-89244-8 (ebook)
[1. Fantasy.] I. Title.
PZ7.D927Dic 2008 [Fic]—dc22 2007047929
ISBN 978-0-375-85572-6 (pbk.)

Printed in the United States of America
30 29 28 27 26 25 24

2016 Yearling Edition

For Jim and Susie,
who made the journey possible

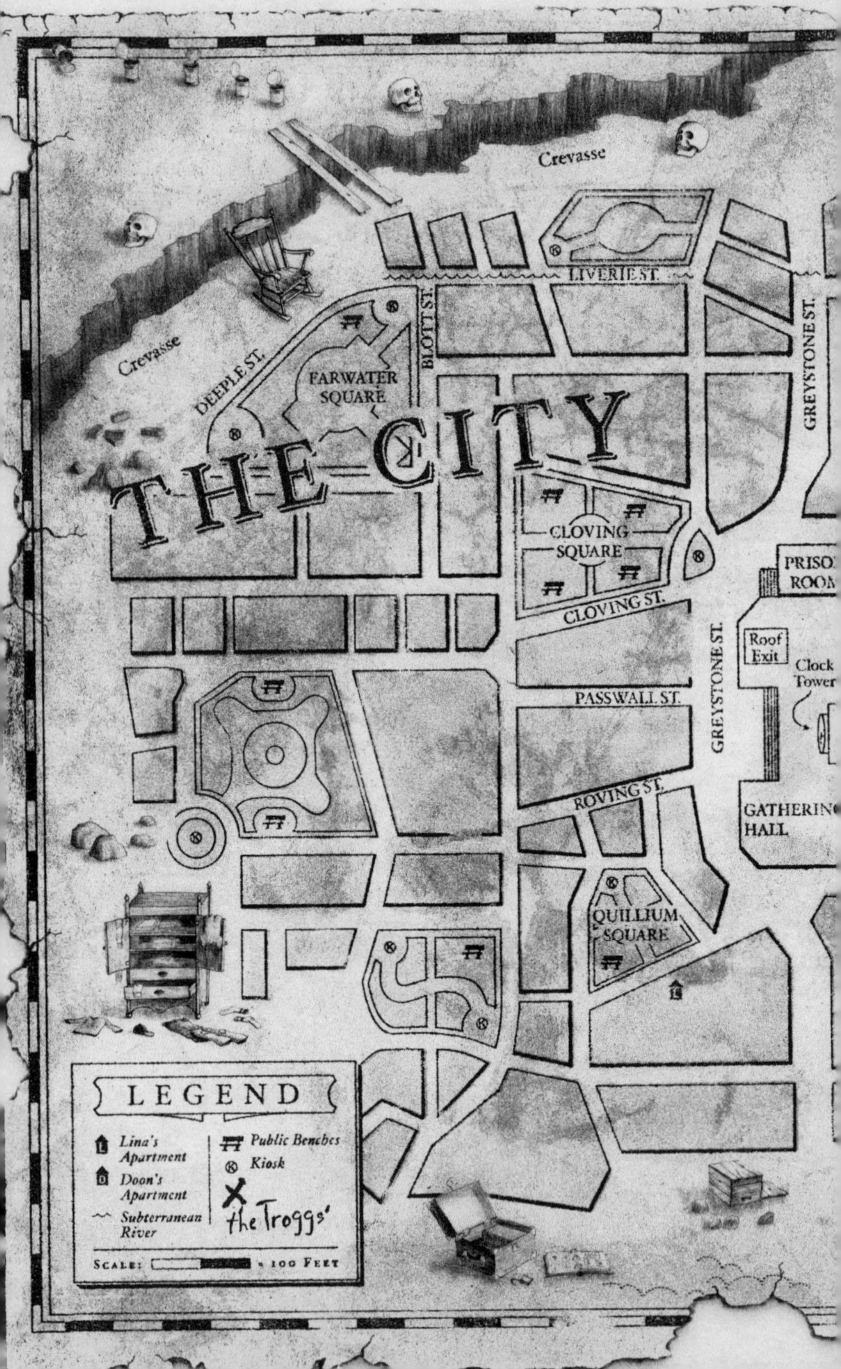
Crevasse
Crevasse
LIVERIE ST.
BLOTT ST.
DEEPLE ST.
FARWATER SQUARE
THE CITY
GREYSTONE ST.
CLOVING SQUARE
CLOVING ST.
PRISO
ROOM
Roof Exit
Clock Tower
PASSWALL ST.
GREYSTONE ST.
ROVING ST.
GATHERIN
HALL
QUILLIUM SQUARE
LEGEND
Lina's Apartment
Doon's Apartment
Subterranean River
Public Benches
Kiosk
the Troggs'
SCALE: = 100 FEET

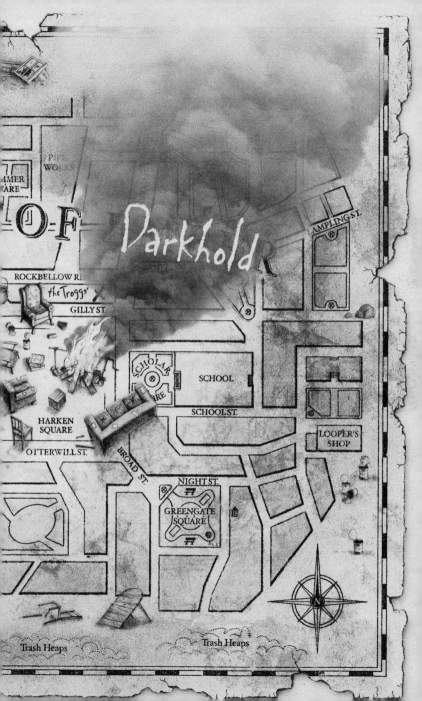

The Vault

Around the middle of the twenty-first century, when it seemed that a great catastrophe was about to engulf the world, an underground city was built as a last refuge for the human race. It was called the city of Ember. The Builders, who designed the city and constructed it, tried to cast their minds into the future—not only to imagine what the residents of the city would need for the many years they'd live there, but also to imagine what life might be like for them when they came back out into the world aboveground. It was this latter question that was on the chief builder's mind on a day when the city was nearly finished and global tensions were rising fast. He summoned his assistant to discuss it.

"When the people emerge from the city," he said, "they will find themselves in a devastated world."

"Unfortunately true," said his assistant.

"Life will be very hard for them," said the chief builder, who was the kind of person who worried about the well-being of others. "I'm wondering if there's something we can do to give them a head start."

The assistant waited, raising his eyebrows politely.

"I have an idea," the chief builder said. "My idea is to give them one thing from today's world—one of our newest inventions—that we know they'll need."

"Excellent," said the assistant, who had no clue what that one thing might be.

"We need a location," the chief builder said, "not far from the exit spot, where we can build a vault into the side of the mountain. We'll put a timed lock on its door, of course, so that it won't be accessible until it should be, just as in our plan for the Instructions for Egress. The vault should be placed so that the citizens of Ember will come across it when they emerge."

"Certainly," said the assistant. He made a note: *Select location.* "But will the people who have lived in Ember know what to do with the . . . um, the contents of the vault?"

"Probably not," said the chief builder. "Naturally, I have thought of that. We'll provide a printed book explaining in detail everything they'll need to know."

"I see," said the assistant. "A good plan."

So it was done. A large, steel-lined room was built into the side of the mountain and stocked according to the chief builder's instructions. Then the door was sealed.

Despite the Builders' fears, the catastrophe did not happen immediately. The midcentury crisis eased. Fifty years later, however, the world came once more to the brink of war, and the government put its plan into action. Volunteers were assembled, couples were formed, and babies were given to each couple. The city of Ember received its first inhabitants.

The bombs fell. Cities burned all over the world. People died in the millions, and plagues and famines and floods reduced even further the numbers of those who were left. It was many, many years before the scattered survivors of the Disaster began to rebuild any sort of civilization.

The people of Ember came out of their underground city somewhat later than planned. Because they were in a state of bewilderment and exhaustion when they emerged, and because trees had grown up where trees hadn't been before, they failed to notice the door to the vault. They trudged away over the hills until they arrived at the village of Sparks, where, after a struggle, they took up their lives anew.

Instead, it was a roamer who discovered the vault. The door wasn't locked; he opened it and went inside, where he found one thing that was interesting, which he took, and one thing that was not interesting: a large, heavy book with small print. Like many people in those times, he had lost the skill of reading. He flipped the book open and scowled at its pages. Should he take it or not? Yes, he decided. He might be able to sell it someday. If not, he could use it for starting fires.

CHAPTER 1

The Storm

In the village of Sparks, the day was ending. The pale winter sun had begun to sink behind a bank of clouds in the west, and shadows darkened the construction field behind the Pioneer Hotel, where workers labored in the gloom. Winter rains had turned the ground to a soup of mud. Stacks of lumber and piles of bricks and stones stood everywhere, along with buckets of nails, tools, old windows and doors, anything that might be useful for building houses. Though the daylight was almost gone, people worked on. They were trying to accomplish as much as possible, because they could see that a storm was coming.

But at last someone called, "Time to quit!" and the workers sighed with relief and began to pack up their tools.

One of the workers was a boy named Doon Harrow, thirteen years old, who had spent the day hauling loads of boards from one place to another and trying to measure and cut them to necessary lengths. When he heard the call, he set down the rusty old saw he'd been using and looked around for his father. The workers stumbling across the field were no more than shadowy figures now; it was hard to tell one from another. Ahead of them loomed the hotel, a few of its windows shining dimly with the light of candles lit by those too young or old or ill to be outside working. "Father!" Doon called. "Where are you?"

His father's voice answered from some distance behind him. "Right here, son. Coming! Wait for—" And then came a sound that made Doon whirl around: first a shattering crash, and then a shriek of a kind he'd never before heard from his mild-mannered father.

Doon ran, squelching through the mud. He found his father sprawled on the ground beside a broken windowpane that had been leaning against a pile of bricks. "What happened?" Doon cried. "Are you hurt?"

His father struggled to his knees. In a hoarse, strangled voice, he said, "Tripped. Fell on the glass. My hand."

Others had gathered now, and they helped him up. Doon took his father's arm. Enough light remained in the sky for him to see what had happened: the palm of his father's hand was sliced open, gushing blood.

One of the men standing nearby tore off his shirt

and wrapped it around the wound. "Make a tight fist," the man said.

Doon's father curled his fingers, wincing. Blood stained the shirt.

"We have to get to the doctor," Doon said.

"Yes, that cut needs stitching up," said the man who'd given his shirt. "Go quick, and maybe you can make it to the village before it rains."

"Can you walk, Father?" Doon asked.

"Oh, yes," said his father in a weak voice. "Might need another . . ." He trailed off, holding out his hand, and Doon saw that the shirt wrapped around it was already soaked with blood.

"Ice would slow the bleeding," someone said. "But we don't have any."

A woman took off her scarf and passed it to Doon, and another man ripped strips of cloth from his shirt. Once the injured hand was wrapped in these, Doon and his father started across the field.

"You'll need a lantern!" cried a boy—one of Doon's friends, Chet Noam. "Go on ahead. I'll get one and catch up with you."

They walked as quickly as they could, but it seemed unlikely they'd avoid getting wet. A few raindrops were already drifting down. Doon felt their light, cold touch on his face. Rain had become familiar to him by now. Since he and his people had arrived here in Sparks from the city of Ember, where sun and rain alike were unknown, four rainstorms had swept over the land. The first had terrified the people of Ember, who thought something dreadful had gone wrong with the sky.

A voice called to them from behind, and Chet came running up. "Here," he said, handing Doon a lantern made of a can punched with holes and containing a burning candle. "And listen," he added. "A roamer has arrived, wanting shelter at the hotel. Tell people that if the rain stops, there'll be trading in the plaza tomorrow morning."

"All right," said Doon. He and his father turned again toward the town and hurried on. "Is the pain very bad?" Doon asked.

"Not too bad," said his father, whose face was unnaturally white. "It *is* bleeding a lot."

"Doctor Hester will know how to stop it," Doon said, though he wasn't sure of that. The doctor did the best she could, but there was a great deal she couldn't cure.

They passed a grove of trees thrashing in the wind. Behind the trees, a little distance off the road, a tall building loomed. A patch of blackness showed where a section of its roof had fallen in.

"They *still* haven't fixed it," said Doon as they went past, but his father didn't even look up.

The damaged building was called the Ark, the

place where the people of Sparks stored their food supplies. The first rainstorm of the winter had been too much for one of the many·rotten spots in its roof. Beams and chunks of tile fell inward. Shelves toppled. Jars and crocks broke and spilled, sacks of grain tore open, and rats got to the food before the cave-in was discovered. Even to begin with, there had been barely enough food stored in the Ark to get everyone through the winter. After that storm, a great part of the food was ruined.

"Father," Doon said. "Press your hurt hand tight with your other hand. That might keep it from bleeding so much." His father nodded and did as Doon said.

The rain came harder. In the last rays of evening light, Doon saw the lines of water like silver pins in the air. He put up the hood of his jacket, shivering. When he was faced with troubles, Doon usually looked for solutions and took action. But tonight he was feeling disheartened. So much about the winter in Sparks had been hard. People were ill with coughs and fevers, and some of them had died; they were hungry nearly all the time; and there had been one accident after another. A candle flame caught a curtain and set a house on fire; a toddler wandered outside at night, fell into the river, and drowned; there was the hole in the Ark's roof; and now this gash in his father's hand. Misfortunes came from every direction, it seemed, and Doon could see no way to make things better.

In a few minutes, they came to the town. People had drawn their curtains and closed their shutters against the wind, so the streets were dark, except for where a narrow line of candlelight showed here and there at a windowsill.

Nearly everyone had gone inside, but they spotted Mary Waters darting from a doorway with her coat pulled up over her head. Doon called to her. "Mary!"

She turned and strode toward them. She was the strongest and most clear-headed of the town's three leaders. Lately, with food supplies so short and a few citizens of Sparks starting to grumble about how everything would be better if those "strangers" were sent away, Mary had stood firm as a rock in defense of the Emberites. "We are *all* the people of Sparks now," she'd declared, again and again. "That's what we decided, and we'll stick to it."

Now she frowned with concern at Loris Harrow's wrapped hand. "What happened?" she asked.

Doon's father explained in a few words. "We're going to the doctor's," said Doon. "And a roamer has just arrived at the Pioneer, so there'll be trading tomorrow if the rain stops."

"Good," said Mary. "Maybe he'll have something we need. Go quick, now; that hand needs attention."

They hurried on, pausing only twice more to mention the roamer to passersby.

The doctor's house was at the far end of town. By the time Doon and his father reached it, the rain was coming down hard. Doon pounded urgently on the door, and in a moment it opened, and there stood Lina Mayfleet, staring at them in astonishment. Her little sister, Poppy, clung to her leg, whimpering. "Oh!" Lina cried. "Come in! What's wrong? You're soaked!"

Just seeing Lina's face, alarmed though it was, made Doon feel a little better. Lina was his closest friend. Together they had found the way out of their dying city of Ember and brought the rest of Ember's people out as well. Doon didn't see Lina very often these days, since he lived at the Pioneer and she lived at Doctor Hester's house. He thought she looked thinner since he'd seen her last.

"I've hurt my hand," Doon's father said. "I need the doctor."

"She's not here," said Lina. "She's with a child who has a fever. But Mrs. Murdo can help."

Mrs. Murdo was at that moment descending the stairs. She had been Lina's neighbor in Ember and now was like a mother to her and Poppy. She peered down, and when she saw Doon and his father, she quickly smoothed her hair and tucked in her shirt. Behind her came Torren, the doctor's nephew, a boy a little younger than Lina, with a narrow face and a tuft of hair that stood up above his forehead as if the wind had

11

lifted it and forgotten to put it back down. The two of them hurried to the new arrivals. Torren's small blue eyes popped with curiosity. "What happened?" he said. "He hurt his hand? Can I see?" He crowded up close to Doon's father. "Eeeww, so much blood!"

"Torren," said Mrs. Murdo, "step aside, please. You and Doon get candles and come with me. Lina, I'll need boiled water and clean rags. This way, Loris. We'll do the best we can until Doctor Hester gets back."

In the doctor's room, Mrs. Murdo sat Doon's father down and had him lay his arm on the table next to him. She bent over his hand. "I wish we had ice," she said. "It might slow the bleeding." But they had none. The last roamer carrying blocks of ice from the mountains had come through town seven weeks ago, and all that he'd brought was long melted. "There are splinters of glass in this cut," Mrs. Murdo said. "Doon and Torren, hold your candles right here so I can see."

Suddenly the windows of the room flashed white. Both Doon and Torren jolted the candles they were holding and dripped hot wax onto Doon's father's hand. Mrs. Murdo cried out, "What was that?" and a second later came a crack and a rumble, like the sky breaking apart.

"It's only lightning," said Torren, as if he hadn't jumped himself. "We're having a thunderstorm."

Doon steadied his hand, but he'd felt a moment of panic at the flash and rumble. He remembered that someone had told him about a thing called lightning—a bolt of electricity that came sometimes in storms. He had not known how to picture a "bolt of electricity." He thought maybe it would be a kind of shudder, like what he'd felt once when he touched the wires of a wall socket back in Ember. Maybe there would be some sparks with it, or some kind of twinkling.

Now, holding his candle over his father's bloody palm, he glanced at the window every time a jagged line of light split the sky from top to bottom. This was a power like nothing he'd ever seen. It struck him through with awe. Somehow, it was electricity. But how could a jagged line of light be the same thing that the old generator in Ember produced from river water? How could something that vanished in an instant be the same thing that made a lamp glow all evening? He saw now that electricity was nothing that people had made; it was part of the world, and sometimes, in some mysterious way, people were able to capture it.

Mrs. Murdo frowned and muttered over her work. "I wish Hester would get here," she said. "I can't see whether I have this properly cleaned. Where's Lina with that water?"

The lightning came again, like a white root shooting down from the clouds. When the thunder followed, Doon felt its rumble deep inside himself, almost like a stern and powerful voice giving him an order he did not understand.

Lina was outside at the backyard pump, pulling the pump handle up and pushing it down, up and down, up and down, making water spurt out to fill the pot and getting splattered by rain the whole time. She felt furiously impatient. In Ember, you turned on a faucet and hot water came right out. If she'd been in Ember now, she'd have had this pot filled in a minute, and she wouldn't be getting wet and cold, and—

At that instant, the whole sky lit up, sudden and brilliant. She staggered backward and cried out, but a terrible roar drowned her voice. Leaving the water pot behind, she fled into the house, and as she crossed the main room, the door burst open and Doctor Hester lurched in, coat flying, scarves whipping around, water streaming from her hair.

"What's happening?" Lina cried. "Is the sky splitting apart?"

The doctor slammed the door behind her, but not before a gust of wind shot in and blew out the fire in the fireplace, leaving the room in darkness. Again the light flashed outside, and again came a deafening bang. Poppy screamed, and Lina ran to pick her up.

"Hester!" Mrs. Murdo called from the other room. "Please come, we need you!"

Another flash of light whitened the windows, followed by a roar.

"Thunderstorm," said the doctor, struggling out of her soaked coat.

"Will it hurt us?" Lina asked, holding tight to Poppy, who was wailing.

"It will if the lightning hits you," the doctor said. "Lightning sets things on fire." She tossed her coat on a chair and hurried off.

Fire from the sky. Lina shuddered. In Ember, the sky never let loose water or ice or stabs of fire; it never made a noise; it was always dark and still and quiet. In Ember, the weather of every day was the same.

The doctor and Mrs. Murdo worked over Loris Harrow's hand for nearly an hour. Doon, Lina, and Torren grew weary from holding the candles to light the operation. Finally, Dr. Hester sighed and stood up. "I *think* we've got all the splinters out," she said. "I just can't see well enough to tell for sure. We'll watch you for signs of infection."

Doon's father smiled faintly. He hadn't cried out as his hand was being probed, but his face was gray. "I know you did the best you could," he said.

"You and Doon must stay here tonight," said Mrs. Murdo. "You can't go out in that storm."

"Thank you," said Doon's father. "We're grateful. And I almost forgot to mention—a roamer is coming into town tomorrow. We may be able to replenish our supplies."

"Maybe," said the doctor. "If we can find anything to trade with."

She made up a bed for Doon's father on the couch. Doon slept on the window seat with an old quilt wrapped around him. Upstairs, Poppy climbed into Lina's bed, too afraid to sleep by herself, and Lina lay listening to the pounding rain and thinking about the city that had been, until just nine months ago, her home.

The city of Ember had been dying. Its food supplies were running out; its buildings were old and crumbling; and worst of all, its electricity was failing. Without electricity, the city would plunge into complete and lasting darkness, because it was under the ground, where no sun shone. The people of Ember hadn't known that, though; Ember had been their entire world.

But as gloomy as Ember had been, it was the place Lina was used to. She missed the job she'd had there, running fast through the streets as a messenger, seeing different places and different people every day. She missed the comfortable apartments where she and Poppy had lived, first with their grandmother and then, after their grandmother died, with Mrs. Murdo.

Ember was a dark place, it was true. But in the daytime, huge lamps lit the streets, and at night—at least until nine o'clock, when the city's electricity was switched off—the houses were cozy and bright inside. You flicked a switch and the lights shone, bright enough to read by, or draw, or play a game of checkers. You didn't have to deal with candle drips or drafts that blew out the flames. You didn't have to constantly feed a fire with wood.

"In winter," Doctor Hester had said to her one recent evening when Lina wanted to draw but they couldn't spare a candle, "we live half our lives in darkness." More than half, Lina had thought. The days were short in winter. Clouds often covered the sun. And the darkness followed you into the house and lurked in corners and up near the ceiling, everywhere the glow of candles and hearthfires didn't reach.

Lina knew it didn't make sense to miss Ember; and yet Ember's dangers were at least familiar. Here they were new and strange. You could be frozen in a snowstorm, blistered by poison oak, attacked by bandits (she'd never seen these, but someone had told her about them), bitten by snakes, or eaten by wild animals. Now there was lightning to add to the list. "Why *are* there so many hard and dangerous things in the world?" Lina once asked Doctor Hester, but the doctor only shrugged.

"It gives us useful work," she said. "There are always going to be people who need help."

But on a night like this, with the sky flaming and roaring and the rain battering down, Lina didn't want to think about useful work. She pulled Poppy close against her. Somewhere far away, she heard a high, eerie howl. Was it the wind? Was it a wanderer lost in the storm? She tugged the covers up over her ears. She felt surrounded by a darkness that was different from the darkness of Ember but just as frightening.

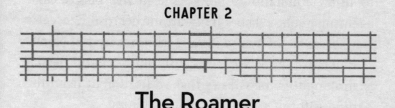

CHAPTER 2

The Roamer

In the morning, Lina woke early, pulled aside the curtain by her bed, and saw that the storm had passed. Her spirits rose. The roamer would come! "Wake up, Poppy," she said, nudging her little sister. "We're going out this morning."

"Nuh-uh," said Poppy into her pillow.

"Yes!" said Lina. "It's going to be exciting! Come on." She got Poppy up and dressed her, and by the time they were downstairs, the rest of the household was up, too.

Mrs. Murdo stirred a pot of corn mush in the kitchen. "Maybe this roamer will have some dried mushrooms," she said. "That would make a nice change. Or some barley. Or walnuts."

"Or just about *anything* different," said Lina, who spent way too much time helping Mrs. Murdo figure out how to make two potatoes feed five people and inventing endless dishes made from corn mush.

"Or some of that willow bark tincture for pain," said Doctor Hester, who was stumbling around blearily, looking for a bag of herbs she'd left somewhere the evening before.

"Yes," said Loris Harrow with a rueful grin. "Could've used that last night."

"Jam!" shouted Torren. "If he has jam, let's get lots of it. I hate eating this icky mush without jam."

They had a hurried breakfast, Doon's father spooning up his mush awkwardly with his left hand, since his right was encased in a bulky bandage. Doon looked as if he hadn't slept much, Lina thought. There were shadows under his eyes.

Getting ready to go out took forever. Poppy spilled a big blob of mush down her front and had to be dressed all over again. Doctor Hester couldn't find her scarf. Torren was rooting around in his box of treasures, looking for something he said was extremely important. Finally, Doon caught Lina's eye and sent her a questioning look. She nodded. "Doon and I will just go on ahead," she said. "Okay?"

Mrs. Murdo waved a hand at them. "Yes, yes, go on."

So the two of them ran out into the windy morning. They headed down the river road and into the muddy streets of the town, where people were streaming toward the plaza to see the roamer.

A roamer was a trader who traveled among the far-flung settlements and into the ruined places to collect goods to trade. The approach of a roamer was always exciting, even at times like these, when people had very little to offer in exchange for whatever goods he might have. Roamers brought news from other villages—crops might be having an especially good or bad year, or sickness might be rampaging, or rivers flooding, or celebrations planned. News came as well from the mountains and from the empty territories that lay between settlements. Roamers could tell people if ice had formed on the lakes, if the wild mushrooms were plentiful, or if there were rumors of bandits. At the very least, an arrival from elsewhere made for a change.

"Let's get up close," Lina said. They edged around the side of the plaza and found a place near the strip of dead brown grass beside the river.

Lina scanned the crowd. Somehow they all looked smaller than they had in the summer, as if they'd been shrunken and withered by the cold. They wrapped their arms tightly across their bodies and drew their shoulders up close to their necks. Their mouths were pinched, their eyes narrow and darting, as if on the alert for the next bad thing that might happen. Lina knew she looked that way, too. She had noticed in the mirror that the bones of her face looked sharper.

She saw Mary Waters, one of the town leaders, gazing at the assembled people with serious eyes, like a mother worried about her children. She spotted her friend Lizzie Bisco standing up on a bench to see out over people's heads. Lizzie had been ill; she was mostly recovered, but her red hair looked dull and tangled, and her face thin. She saw Kenny Parton waving at Doon and making his way toward them; he was a shy, quiet boy who seemed to amuse himself mostly by wandering around noticing things. He had become a friend of Doon's toward the end of the summer, when something he'd noticed had given Doon an important bit of information about a treacherous young man named Tick. A few minutes later, Torren came running into the plaza like mad, holding something in front of him in both hands. Behind him, Mrs. Murdo bustled along, carrying a basket of dried garlic.

They waited. People talked in low voices, shivering, breathing clouds in the cold air. They turned up their collars against the knife-edged wind that whistled around the corners of the shops; they pulled their hats and scarves over their ears. A great many of them coughed and wiped runny noses on their sleeves; the cold and damp had spread illness through the town, and illness took a harsh toll on people who were weak to begin with from having too little to eat. Three people, so far, had died of fevers the doctor couldn't cure. Lina had watched through the back window of the house as their wooden coffins—two big ones and one very small one—had been carried toward the town's cemetery.

Finally, a creaking and clanking signaled that the roamer was near. Lina stood on tiptoe, trying to see. But what appeared around the corner of the town hall was not quite what she had expected. For one thing, the roamer was a woman—a short, stout, ruddy-faced woman with hair like broom bristles, dusty yellow, chopped off roughly just below her ears. Her clothes were tattered and grimy, hardly more than rags stitched crudely together, lashed around with straps and cords from which hung a couple of knives and a battered tin bottle and a pair of scissors. She walked ahead of her wagon, carrying a long stick in one hand.

The wagon was covered with an odd tent made of patches of different colors. All the patches were faded and dirty, but still the tent had a dull shine, like a cracked old raincoat. As its owner did, the wagon had things hanging off it—pots and pans, cloth sacks and leather pouches, coils of rope, buckets. A few sheep shambled along behind, not white and fluffy but gray as dishrags.

The animal pulling the wagon was a kind Lina had never seen before. It was much more slender than an ox—probably too slender, since its ribs showed in ridges along its sides. It had long thin legs, a curtain of hair on its neck, and ears that pointed upward. It turned its long face to look at the crowd.

"Hey, a horse," said Kenny Parton, who was

standing with Lina and Doon. "We hardly ever get to see them."

She didn't know why, but Lina loved that horse as soon as she saw it. She had no idea what horses were like. Maybe they were terrible, savage animals. This one certainly looked strong enough to give a person a deadly kick; maybe it would bite. It threw its head up all of a sudden and made a noise, and she saw its rows of teeth. But somehow she loved it anyway.

The roamer had halted her wagon and was starting to speak. "Come in close!" she cried. "Gather round! I have things to sell. High-quality, unusual things! Bargain prices!"

People pushed up closer.

"Look at my fine sheep!" the roamer called. "I'm selling just one today." She turned around and hustled behind the sheep, shooing them forward. "Go on, lambies," she said, nudging their rear ends with her stick. The sheep skittered forward, bleating. "See how fat they are? See how healthy? Great for wool, great for tallow, great for stew!"

Even Lina, who was no judge of animals, could tell that these sheep were not especially fine. In fact, they looked rather ill. Their wool was matted, and their legs were dark with mud.

"Who'll buy a sheep?" the roamer cried. "I'll sell one for five bags of corn or four bags of beans. Make me an offer!"

No one spoke up. Sparks didn't have any bags of beans or corn to spare.

The roamer scowled. "Come on!" she yelled. "There's nothing wrong with 'em! You'd be a little grubby, too, if you'd been up in the mountains half the winter. Give 'em a good wash and they'll be just fine."

Still no offers came from the crowd.

So the roamer shrugged angrily and reached into the back of her wagon. She brought out some bags and boxes. "All right," she said. "Other items of interest. Best offer accepted. Edibles especially favored. Also candles." One by one, she held them up.

There was a rusted bucket, a handful of old coins, a few straps and belts, a thick brown glass bottle. . . . Hattie Carranza, standing next to Lina, sighed and shook her head. "This is the most pathetic batch of junk I've ever seen," she said.

A few of the things found takers. Martha Parton offered a small jar of squash pickles for a battered cooking pot; old Ferny Joe traded a sack of dried prunes for a carved walking stick. When the roamer held up a tiny plastic figurine—it seemed to be a little man with big muscles—Torren piped up with an offer for it, saying he had something extremely old and extremely special, a real remote with fourteen buttons. But the roamer just flapped her hand, dismissing him. "Edibles, I said. Can't eat that useless thing."

Torren frowned furiously. The remote was one of

his treasures. He also had toy versions of a tank, a motorcycle, and an elephant; he had a nonworking flashlight; and—best of all—he had forty-eight real light bulbs that his brother Caspar had brought him from his roamings. He'd even seen one of them lit up once, when Doon connected it to the little generator he'd made. His light bulbs were his favorite treasure. He wasn't about to give *them* up. But he'd thought for sure he'd be able to buy something with the remote, which he didn't care that much about, because he didn't really know what it was.

Soon no more offers came from the villagers. People began to drift away, disappointed. The roamer, seeing this, banged her stick on the wheel of her wagon and raised her voice. "News!" she cried. "I've got two pieces of news. You can have 'em for cheap."

Of course, everyone was interested in news. Usually roamers told the news for free, but this one clearly wasn't giving anything away. Mary Waters stepped forward and told her she could have five candles for her news.

"All right!" the roamer cried.

Everyone grew quiet.

"First thing is," said the roamer, "there's a pack of wolves in the area. I've seen the big birds circling. So keep a good watch on your sheep and goats."

People frowned and murmured to each other

about flocks and fences. Lina turned to Kenny. "Are wolves big birds?" she asked him.

"Nope," he said. "They're dogs, sort of, only more fierce. They howl. It's like they sing together. In hard winters, they come in closer to where people live and they kill animals. People, too, sometimes. Then the birds come in later to pick over what's left."

With a shiver, Lina added wolves to her ever-growing list of the world's dangers.

"Second thing is," the roamer was saying, jabbing a finger at the sky, "a new star is up there. It moves, is the odd thing about it. I've seen it myself."

The villagers murmured a bit about this. Lina heard a couple of people saying they'd seen the same thing. "It's not right," someone said. "Stars shouldn't move."

The roamer started putting her things back into their bags and boxes.

"I know how to make a wolf-scaring whistle," Kenny said to Doon. "Want me to show you?"

But Doon didn't answer. Lina saw that he was staring at something the roamer hadn't offered for sale. It lay near the rear wheel of her wagon. It looked to her like a flopped-open book lying on its face.

The rest of the crowd left, and Kenny wandered off, too. Doon beckoned Lina to come with him and stepped up to the roamer. "What's that?" he asked, pointing to the book.

She glanced back. "Oh, that," she said. "I use it for my fires."

"What are you asking for it?" Doon said.

She turned from her task of bundling and boxing. "You *want* it?" A gleam appeared in her eye. "Of course, it might be very valuable," she said. "Ancient as it is. Discovered high up in the mountains, under unusual circumstances."

"Oh, I don't think it's valuable," said Doon. "I just happen to be a book collector. I could pay . . . um . . . let me see. I don't have anything with me right now," he said. "But I could get . . . I could get some . . ." He hesitated, thinking, eyeing the tattered book longingly.

Lina could see that he wanted it. The book was a mess, falling apart. But she knew how Doon felt about books.

She had an idea. "I'll buy it for you," she said to him. She turned to the roamer. "I'll give you a match for it."

"A what?" said the roamer.

"A match," said Lina. "You know, to make fire." She happened to have three of them in her pocket. She carried them around with her because she so often needed one—to light a candle, to light the fire in the stove, to lend to a neighbor whose fire had gone out. All the matches in Sparks had been brought there by the people from Ember; to the villagers, they were wonderful things. The plan had been to save them for trading, to help buy food and supplies now that the town's population had grown; but when the cold weather came, people couldn't resist using matches to start their fires. It was so much easier than using the flint-stones. Probably, Lina thought, the matches were nearly gone by now.

The shepherd's eyebrows shot up. "Really? I've heard of those match things, but I've never—" Then quickly she put on her cagey expression again. "I mean, *really?* You're offering me just *one?* For this extremely ancient and important book? I think three would be more like it."

Lina glanced at Doon.

"Never mind, then," he said.

"All right, all right," the roamer said quickly. "Two."

"One," Lina said. "That book is in terrible shape." She took a match from her pocket and offered it. The roamer shrugged and gave Doon the book, smirking, clearly thinking she had gotten the better deal.

Doon picked up the book. Lina saw right away that it was in ruins—the roamer had torn out so many of its pages that the cover's edges clapped together. Some torn strips still remained near the book's spine, where the roamer had ripped pages out unevenly, but there seemed to be only a very few pages left whole, and even those were stained and warped. That was a waste of a good match, Lina thought.

Doon turned the book over in his hands and

looked at its cover. Then he looked up at the roamer. "You got this up in the mountains?"

"Yep. Right near a—" She clapped a hand over her mouth and cackled. "But he told me not to tell," she said between her grubby fingers.

"Near what?" Doon demanded. "*Who* told you not to tell?"

The roamer just grinned and shook her head. She tossed the last of her trading goods back into the wagon, and as she worked, she hummed a little tune—a tune that somehow sounded familiar to Lina, though she didn't know why. When the bags and boxes were all stowed away, the roamer took hold of the horse's harness.

"Wait," Lina said. "May I touch that horse?"

The roamer looked surprised, but she nodded. Lina patted the horse's shaggy side, and it rolled its big eye at her and huffed gently through its black nose holes. She combed her fingers through the tangled hair on its neck; she reached up high and stroked its soft ear.

"When he was young," said the roamer, "I used to ride him."

"*Ride?* You mean you got on his back? Does he go fast?"

"He used to," said the roamer, giving the horse a couple of pats.

"Faster than a bicycle?" asked Lina.

The roamer laughed. "Faster than the water in

the river." Then she tugged the reins, and the horse picked up a lanky leg and started forward. The roamer, leading the horse, walked away. Her sheep straggled behind.

Lina was about to say goodbye to Doon, but he took hold of her arm. "Lina," he said, "look at this." There was something in his voice that made her turn to him in surprise. He held out the book, showing her the cover. "Directions for Use," it said in large print.

"Use of what?" said Lina. "I don't understand."

"No, look down here," said Doon, pointing at smaller print at the cover's lower edge.

Lina peered at it. "For the people from Em," it said, and then there was a blot of something on the last part of the word. But it didn't matter. She knew what the word was. She looked up at Doon, wide-eyed.

"Ember," they said, both speaking at the same time.

CHAPTER 3

The Book of Eight Pages

The next morning, Doon showed up at the door of the doctor's house, looking for Lina. "She's out in back," said Mrs. Murdo, "hanging up the wash."

Doon found her in the midst of clothes and covers flapping in the chilly wind. She was hoisting things up over a cord strung between the house and a tree, pinning them in place with split sticks. "Lina," he said. "I have to talk to you."

She came out from behind a large damp skirt (one of Doctor Hester's). "Good," she said. "What have you figured out?" The day before, after they'd recognized the word "Ember" on the cover, Doon had gone quickly back home to read through what was left of the book's pages.

"It's definitely something from the ancient world," he said now, "but I can't tell exactly what. You know how many pages are left in this book? Eight! And most of them are from the back. That roamer must have started tearing them out one by one from the beginning. But the back pages are mostly diagrams and math and words I don't understand."

"Can you understand *any* of it?" Lina asked, pulling a wet shirt out of the laundry basket.

"Just a little, here and there, but it's enough to give me a few clues. I think the book must be about a machine of some sort, maybe something electric. I can make out the word 'current,' for instance. Doesn't that sound like electricity?"

"I don't know," said Lina. "It could mean the current of a river." Doon was so fascinated by electricity that anything could sound electric to him, she thought.

"There's also 'crystal' and 'shine,'" Doon said.

Lina flopped the shirt over the clothesline. "That sounds more like jewels."

"No, I don't think so," Doon said. "I think it's some kind of machine." He seemed full of pent-up energy. He paced back and forth beside the clothesline, batting the windblown clothes out of his way. "I just know that book is important, Lina," he said. "And it was meant for us! For the people from Ember."

Lina was trying to pin the shirt to the line, but the wind kept snatching it away from her. "Would you help me with this shirt? I can't make it stay up."

Doon grabbed one sleeve of the shirt and wrapped it around the clothesline. "I've been thinking so much about all this, Lina. About this book and what it might mean and about what happened to the Ark and how I'd like to . . ." He trailed off. The shirt came loose from the line and fell into the dirt before Lina could catch it. "I don't *know* for sure," Doon went on, not noticing. "But I feel . . ." He looked away, and his eyebrows drew together as if he were figuring out a puzzle written in the sky. "I feel the way we did about the Instructions that Poppy chewed up. It was our mystery to figure out. It came to *us*. This feels the same."

Lina, picking up the shirt and shaking the dirt off it, thought of the tattered book with dismay. "You mean we have to figure out what it says? What all those missing pages are about?"

"No, no, we can't do that. Too much is gone. But we have to do *something*. We can't just ignore it." The wind blew his hair into his eyes, and he swiped it away impatiently. "There are so many troubles here, Lina. It's cold and dark, and there isn't enough food, and people are sick. . . . Maybe the book is about something that would make things better."

"Did you show it to your father?"

"No," Doon said. "I haven't shown it to anyone."

"Why not?"

Doon went on as if he hadn't heard this question. "I think there's something up near Ember that we were meant to find. Look at the title of the book: 'Directions for Use.' It's so much like 'Instructions for Egress'!"

"It is," Lina admitted.

"I think we should go and look for it," Doon said.

Lina gave a short laugh of disbelief. "No one would let us," she said.

"I know. That's why I haven't told anyone. We'd be forbidden to go."

"But how *can* we go?" asked Lina. "We don't even know what we'd be looking for." An uneasy feeling twisted in her stomach. She wasn't sure if it was excitement or fear.

"I've been thinking and thinking about it," Doon said. "I know it's risky. We might not find anything at all. But I want to go back to Ember, Lina. And I want you to come with me."

But of course that was impossible. Lina had tried to laugh when Doon said it, but she couldn't quite laugh, because she saw that he was serious. She could tell that he would have explained all his plans to her right there, in the cold yard with the laundry flying, if Mrs. Murdo hadn't called out the kitchen window for Lina to come in and peel potatoes. "Meet me tomorrow," Doon said. "At the Ark, at sunrise. Can you? I'll tell you more then."

She agreed. That afternoon, as she peeled potatoes, fetched wood for the fire, dug a hole in the garden for the garbage, and scraped up wax drippings to melt down for more candles, she was too busy to do much thinking. But in the evening, she finally had time to be still. Dinner was over. It hadn't been much of a dinner—just a thin carrot soup, dry bread, and some bits of cheese with the mold cut off. Lina had gotten used to having a half-empty stomach most of the time.

She settled herself in a chair by the fire. Torren was sitting on the floor nearby, poking the logs with a long fork and watching the sparks fly up. Poppy was asleep upstairs. On the table beside Lina was an unfinished drawing she'd been working on for weeks in her brief spare moments. She'd always loved to draw. When she'd lived in Ember, she had drawn pictures of a city that she saw in her imagination—a bright, beautiful city not like Ember at all, with white buildings and a blue sky. It was just a dream, she knew, something she'd made up (she'd never seen a sky that wasn't black), but it held a fascination for her, and she drew it over and over. She had left those pictures behind when she left Ember. She wished she still had them, and she'd tried once or twice to draw them again. But it didn't work somehow. These days, she wanted to draw what she saw around her—the houses and animals and trees of Sparks.

The drawing she'd been working on lately was of a chicken. It wasn't coming out well. Most of the time, she had to use bits of charcoal for drawing, so her pictures turned out clumsy and smeared. Now and then,

Doon found a pencil stub for her at the hotel, which let her draw clear lines for a while. But she missed the colored pencils she'd had in Ember. They would have been perfect for this chicken picture.

Her paper came from Doon, too. He had been working with Edward Pocket, who'd been the librarian in Ember. Here in Sparks, Edward had put himself in charge of the huge disorderly pile of books that had accumulated over the years in the back room of the Ark. Little by little, with Doon's help, he was putting these books in order so that people could actually find them and read them. Doon had discovered that old books sometimes had blank pages in the back. He tore them out and brought them to Lina.

She turned her thoughts to Ember. The very name filled her with both sadness and longing. Ember, where she had grown up, where all the people she cared about had lived. Ember, whose streets and buildings she had known so well, every alley, every corner, every doorway. She thought about what Doon had said. Could she go back there? Would she want to?

Mrs. Murdo came in with a candle in one hand and a cup of tea in the other—mint, Lina could tell from the scent of it. She sank into a chair by the dying fire. "Doctor Hester's asleep," she said. "I finally convinced her she needed to rest. She's been rushing around taking care of everyone else for weeks, and she's worn herself out."

To Lina, a room always felt more safe and comfortable when Mrs. Murdo was in it. She was a neat, upright, sharp-featured woman, not the soft and cozy sort at all, but she was kind and sensible, and Lina trusted her completely.

"We should get to bed," said Mrs. Murdo.

"I don't want to go to bed," said Torren. He hunched up his shoulders and pinched his face into a frown.

"You'll want to after the fire burns down and it gets cold," said Mrs. Murdo.

"I'll go then," said Torren. "Not now." He prodded the burnt logs with the fork until they fell into glowing pieces.

"Embers," Lina said, looking at them. "That's what our city was named after."

"I don't see how you could have lived underground," said Torren. "I still think you might be making it all up."

"We're not," said Lina. "Why would we?"

"Maybe you really came from outer space," Torren said. "On an airplane."

"You were *there* when we came," Lina said. "Did you notice any airplane?"

"No," Torren said. He swept the fork around in the fireplace, scattering the coals. "I'd just like to *see* that underground place, that's all."

Maybe I would, too, thought Lina. But when she

thought about how Ember would be now—completely dark, completely abandoned—she shivered. No, they couldn't possibly go. She would say that to Doon tomorrow, and surely he would come to his senses and agree.

She went down to the Ark early the next morning. It was a blustery day. Clouds rose from the western horizon, immense, looking like carved wood painted white with blue shadows. Up on the roof of the main part of the building, workers were ripping away rotted, sodden wood, hurrying to repair the hole before the next rain. The roof of the back room, where Edward Pocket was making his library, hadn't been damaged, and some people had grumbled about that. Why couldn't the useless books have gotten ruined instead of the food?

Doon was standing outside the back room door. The wind flapped his jacket. He wasn't wearing the old brown jacket he'd always worn before. In just the last month or so, that one had gotten impossibly small for him, and he now had a dark green one that came from the donation pile the people of Sparks had put together for their new citizens. It was a bit frayed around the cuffs, but at least his bare wrists didn't poke out from the sleeves.

"Come inside," Doon said, "out of the wind." He led her into the back room, where a giant heap of books had accumulated over the years. They picked their way among the tumbled piles in the dim light coming from the one dirty window. Doon made two book stacks for them to sit on. Before Lina could say anything, he began explaining. "I know you think I've lost my mind," he said.

"Well," Lina said, "I do think so, sort of. I don't see how we could find our way to Ember. Even if we could, it would take too long to get there—we'd have to be out in the cold at night. It took us four days to get to Sparks after we came out of Ember."

"But you and I could go much faster," Doon said. "When we came from Ember, we had old people and small children with us, and we didn't know where we were going. You and I could do it in one long day's walk, I'm sure."

"But even if we could get there," said Lina, "we couldn't get into the city. We couldn't go against the current up the river."

"I know," said Doon. "But we might be able to get in from above. I'm thinking we could go back to that ledge we threw the message from. We could check the slope of the cliff. Maybe we could get down it."

"But even if we could get down," Lina said, "the city's completely dark. We'd never find anything there—even if we *did* know what we were looking for."

"But we have candles now," Doon said. "We'll take lots of them with us. I'll study every word of that book for clues about what we're looking for and where it is.

And listen—we might not find the thing in the book, but we could find other things. There might still be food there. Or medicine. Remember that salve we used to rub on cuts? If some of that was left, it could help my father. He won't say so, but I can tell his hand hurts him terribly. It might be infected."

"I remember that salve," Lina said. "It was called Anti-B. I think we still had an old tube of it at Granny's, mostly empty."

"Even a little would help," Doon said. "And there might be other useful things people could trade with. We could find out."

Lina could see how excited he was, how much he wanted to do this. To her it seemed dangerous, difficult, and probably hopeless. But she had to admit that his excitement inspired her a bit. Life had been hard and dull lately; an adventure would change that. She wasn't a bit sure that Doon's plans would succeed. Things were always so much neater in a person's imagination than they were in real life. But just to go on a journey, even if they found nothing and had to turn right around and come home . . . She was tempted.

"But we can't just disappear," Lina said. "People would worry." She remembered how terribly anxious Mrs. Murdo had been the two times before when she'd gone away without saying where she was going: when she left Ember on the day of the Singing, and just a few months ago when she went off to the ancient ruined city. She didn't want to put Mrs. Murdo through that again.

But Doon had all this figured out, too. It was complicated, but he was sure it would work. Lina, he said, must go and talk to Maddy. She was the one who'd come to town during the summer with Torren's brother, Caspar, and stayed on, after Caspar's quest failed, to help with the garden. There wasn't much to do on the garden in winter, so Maddy would have extra time. Lina should ask her if she'd be willing to move to the doctor's house for a few days and help Mrs. Murdo. If Maddy said yes—Doon was sure she would—Lina should tell Mrs. Murdo that she needed a bit of a change and would like to stay at the Pioneer for a while. "Tell her that you and Maddy will just switch places," he said. "Then, once Maddy has left, I'll tell my father I'm going to stay with you at the doctor's house for a few days because you need some extra help."

"But won't your father wonder why we need Maddy *and* you?" Lina asked.

"No. With so many people sick and the doctor always away, he'll know she needs lots and lots of help."

The sun went behind a cloud, and the light in the room grew even dimmer than before. Lina pondered. Her sensible self and her adventurous self tugged against each other. She looked at the serious expression in Doon's dark eyes. He was determined to do this. She wasn't sure if he was being brave or reckless, wise or foolish. Maybe a little of each.

"So," Doon said, "shall we go?"

She thought of the empty lands, the wolves that ranged there, the rain and cold and wind. She thought of peeling potatoes, cleaning the outhouse, washing medicine bottles, hanging up laundry. She thought of Ember, where—just possibly—something important might be waiting for them. She pushed her doubts aside and took a deep breath.

"All right," she said. "We'll go."

Doon nodded, not smiling. "I knew you'd say that."

CHAPTER 4

Plans for a Journey

"All right," said Doon. He leaned forward, elbows on his knees. Behind him, dust particles hung in the light from the window. "Now, this is my plan. We'll leave three days from now, as long as it's a clear day. If it isn't, we'll have to wait—we can't risk getting caught in rain or snow. We'll go as early in the morning as we can, just before the sun comes up, and we'll walk fast and steadily all day. That should get us there by evening. We'll camp for the night inside the cave entrance. We'll have blankets to keep us warm. We could make a fire in there. And then in the morning we'll explore. We'll see if it's possible to go into the city."

"And then what?" Lina asked.

"By then," said Doon, "I will have studied that book. I'll know what we should do."

"But Doon, what if you can't figure out any clues?

There's the whole huge dark city, hundreds of rooms, all the storerooms, the Pipeworks. . . ."

"I know, I know," Doon said. "If I can't find clues in the book, we'll look to see if there's food and supplies, enough to help Sparks through the winter. There might be! People left food behind in their kitchens. There's probably still a little in the storerooms. The mayor had his hoard. You never know what we might find."

"Hmm," Lina said doubtfully.

Doon went on. "We'll spend one day in the city, camp again that night, and then we'll come back the next day." He finished with a brisk nod.

Lina could tell he was pleased by his plan and eager to carry it out. "Well, maybe—" she said.

Doon stood up and flung his hands out. *"Lina!"* he cried, clearly exasperated. "People are in trouble here and we might be able to help! What if we find canned food? What if we find medicine for my father's hand? And besides." He paused, and his eyes gleamed. "We have a book called *For the People from Ember*! There's something up there *for us*. How could we not go looking for it?"

"You're right," she said. Again came the darting feeling that could have been either excitement or fear. "But just in case something goes wrong," she added, "someone should know where we really are. I'll leave a note for Mrs. Murdo—somewhere she won't find it until we're gone."

Doon agreed. Then he took a piece of paper from his pocket. "I've made a list of things we need to take with us," he said. He handed the paper to Lina. She read through it. The list was long: warm clothes, a blanket, candles, matches, dried food, bottles for water. . . . Lina read on.

"You'll need a pack you can carry on your back," Doon said. "Can you make one?"

"I guess so," Lina said.

"We'll meet in three days," Doon said. "Where the river road goes out into the fields, at the north end of town."

"All right," Lina said. She saw in Doon the determination he'd had on that last day of school in Ember, when everything began, when he'd thrown down his job assignment and outraged the mayor, when he'd shouted out that the city was headed for disaster unless something was done. He wasn't shouting now. But he had that same fierce look in his eyes.

At that moment, the door opened, and Edward Pocket came in. "Aha," he said. "Do I have two helpers this morning instead of only one?"

Doon said, "No, I just had to talk to Lina for a minute; she's going."

"Don't you want to see my latest find first?" Edward

said. He rummaged through a heap of books near the door and brought out one with a bent purple cover. "I read this yesterday," he said. "It's one of the strangest yet." He showed them the title: *Famous Fairy Tales.* "I read the whole thing," Edward said, "but I'm still not sure what a fairy is. Some sort of combination of a person and an insect, I think. The strangest things happen in these stories."

"Like what?" Lina asked, peering at the pages of the book as Edward flipped through it. There were pictures, and if she hadn't been in the middle of such an important conversation with Doon, she would have liked to look at them.

"Oh," said Edward, "mostly terrible things. People turn into frogs, or go to sleep for a thousand years, or fight with huge lizards. I doubt that these things are true. But even if they are, everything almost always turns out quite well. Nearly all the stories have the same last sentence: 'They lived happily ever after.' Of course, that can't be true, either."

"It can't?" Lina said. It sounded lovely to her: happily ever after.

Doon was jiggling a foot impatiently.

"Of course not," said Edward, "unless this world we're in now works in a whole different way from the one where we used to live."

"Lina," said Doon. "I'll walk out with you."

"May I borrow that book sometime?" Lina asked

Edward. He said of course she could, and she thanked him and went outside with Doon.

"So we'll meet in three days," Doon said once they were several steps away from the door. "We'll go early, *really* early, before anyone is up. Can you be there just before sunrise?"

"I'll be there," Lina said. It will be all right, she told herself. We'll be gone only a few days. It will be fine.

It was easy to get Maddy to come help Mrs. Murdo. When Lina found her, she was by the riverbank, making her way slowly along, head down. Maddy was the kind of person who seems scary at first. She was big, and she didn't smile much, and she wasn't in the least chatty. But Lina had learned that there was kindness behind Maddy's stern appearance, so she approached her now without hesitation.

Maddy was wearing a green cape that made her look even larger than she was. Her wild swirl of red-brown hair fell in tangles on either side of her face. She glanced up when she heard Lina coming, nodded, and went back to her task.

"I'm gathering round lettuce," she said when Lina asked what she was doing. She showed Lina a basket full of small round leaves. "It's good for you, and it doesn't taste too bad."

When Lina explained about needing a change and

asked Maddy if she'd trade places with her for a few days, Maddy said right away that she would. "There isn't much going on here except building right now," she said. "And building is not my specialty." So they arranged it: in three days, Maddy and Lina would change places.

Persuading Mrs. Murdo was a little harder. She didn't understand why Lina would choose this difficult time to go away.

"But it's *because* it's a difficult time," Lina said, following after Mrs. Murdo as she went from one task to another—poking the fire, sweeping dirt out the door, wringing out clothes that had been soaking in a bucket. "I need a break from it. And Maddy needs a change, too. She'll be just as much of a help as me. More, even."

"Maddy is a capable person, it's true," Mrs. Murdo conceded, scraping candle drippings from the table.

"It's only for a few days," said Lina. She gave Mrs. Murdo her best pleading look, although there was still a little bit of her that wished to be forbidden, so she wouldn't have to go.

But Mrs. Murdo gave in. So there would be no backing out, and Lina began to get ready. For the next three days, she spent a lot of time trying to do things without being noticed. She said she was tired and went to her room to work on sewing sacks together to make a backpack. She kept a sharp eye out for everyone's comings and goings, and when no one was around, she took candles and matches from the cupboard. She took ten matches, hoping that Mrs. Murdo, who was very good at keeping the fire going, wouldn't notice.

Two nights before they were to leave, she wrote the note for Mrs. Murdo:

Doon and I have gone back to Ember to find something important. We have a good plan, don't worry. We'll be back in just a few days.
Love, Lina

She folded the note up small and buried it in the middle of a tub of dried beans in the kitchen. Mrs. Murdo used these beans for soup, but she wasn't likely to use half the tub before Lina and Doon got back.

After that, she had one more night of restless, wakeful sleep, and in the morning, loaded with a heavy backpack full of all the things on Doon's list, she crept out of the house in the early darkness, long before anyone else was stirring. She paid a brief visit to the stinky, spidery outhouse in the backyard (in Ember, toilets were *inside* the house, right down the hall from the bedroom), and then she headed up the road. Stars shone in the black sky, and the ground, stiff with frost, crunched under her feet. When she got to the far end of the river road, she saw a shadowy figure. It was Doon, waiting for her. She hurried up to him. He had a pack on his back, and he was wearing his frayed green jacket and dark pants, but there was a dash of brightness about him, too—an orange scarf wrapped around his neck. Somehow it made him look ready for adventure.

"There you are," Doon whispered, even though there was no one anywhere around.

Lina whispered, too. "I'm here. I'm ready, I think."

"All right," said Doon. "Let's go."

CHAPTER 5

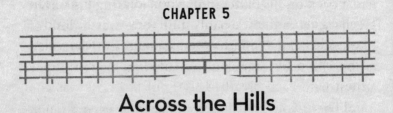

Across the Hills

They set out, walking side by side. The starlight was enough to see by, at least while they were still on the road. No moon shone. The moon had disappeared in the way it did every now and then; Lina wasn't sure why. It grew from a silver sliver to a silver circle and shrank back into a sliver and disappeared, and it did this over and over. When she asked Doctor Hester why, she said, "It's because of the earth's shadow," but the doctor was in a tearing hurry that day, rushing off to help someone who'd cut himself with his axe, and that was all she said before dashing out the door.

The night was utterly still except for their footsteps on the road. No birds sang at this hour. On the left, the black bare branches of the trees stood against the slightly lighter black of the sky. On the right, the fields stretched away, scattered with the dead tomato vines that had been left to lie where they fell after the harvest.

For a while, Lina and Doon didn't speak. They walked quickly and steadily until they were beyond the last fields and the last outlying houses of the village. Lina could feel the cold air traveling down into her chest with each breath. The tip of her nose was cold, and the tops of her ears. She pulled the knitted hat she was wearing farther down. It was thrilling to be out this early, starting an adventure, striding along through the darkness with Doon. But still a sense of uneasiness stayed with her, like something growling softly in the pit of her stomach.

After a while, the sky behind the distant mountains faded to a lighter shade of black, and then to a shade lighter still, and then to a beautiful deep blue-green.

"The sun's coming up," Lina said.

They watched as they walked. A brightness appeared above the line of the hills, first a dim orange and then a blazing yellow, until at last the gold eye of the sun sailed up from wherever it had been and the whole world filled with light.

Lina took a long deep breath. "It's so beautiful, isn't it, Doon? Even in winter, when everything is brown and gray, this place is still beautiful."

Doon gazed out across the grassy meadow to where the trees began at its farthest edge. "It's beautiful," he said, "but hard to live in. Are things so hard everywhere, I wonder? Maybe there are places in the world where life is easier."

"Where people live happily ever after," Lina said, thinking of the book Edward had shown them. Maybe this quest they were on would bring happily-ever-after to Sparks.

Doon shaded his eyes with one hand and squinted upward. "We need to go northeast now," he said, "toward the mountains. Remember how we came across the squash fields when we arrived here? They're over that way."

The going was harder after they left the road. Their feet turned on the rough clumps of earth, and mud clung to their shoes. Soon the way began to slope upward, and a while later they came to the top of the first ridge of hills.

Lina stopped here and turned around. "This is where we first saw the town," she said. "Remember?"

They gazed down at it. It looked very different now from when they'd seen it that first time, nine months ago. Then a carpet of green had covered the hills, and the little buildings had looked peaceful beside their thriving fields. Now the fields were bare, and a haze of smoke hung in the air. The houses and shops had a huddled look, as if they were crowding together to keep warm.

They walked for a long time, perhaps an hour, perhaps more. Soon, Lina thought, we should come to the road we walked along when we came out of Ember, the road that ran alongside a stream. But there was no sign of it yet—only, in all directions, the gray-brown grass, the gray-green oak trees, and the small groves of trees with no leaves at all.

"I know we came this way," Doon said, as if he were reading her thoughts. "Because look—even though it's been so long, you can still see the path our feet trampled."

It was true. You couldn't see it very clearly, but if you looked hard, there it was: a wide strip of ground where the grass had not simply fallen or been blown sideways by the wind, but was flattened by the tread of eight hundred feet. It was like the ghost of a road, winding across the landscape. They followed it. Lina kept her eyes on a clump of oak trees in the distance that was shaped a bit like a hand in a mitten. Watching the trees gradually get closer was a way to tell they were making progress.

"So," said Lina, "tell me what you've figured out from the book."

Doon said nothing. He tramped on as if he hadn't heard her, frowning at the ground. So Lina asked her question again, louder. "Doon! Did the book give you some clues?"

Doon sighed. "Well, not really," he said. "I wish I'd gotten that roamer to tell me where she found it. I don't know if it was *in* Ember or *outside* of Ember."

"And did you figure out what the book is about?"

"Well, it's directions for something, we know that. But I still can't tell exactly what."

"Did you bring it with you?"

Doon nodded. "The trouble is, there's so much missing. The book doesn't even begin until page forty-seven—all the pages before that have been torn out."

"What's on page forty-seven?" Lina asked.

"Just two words: 'Technical Information.'"

"What does 'technical' mean?"

"I think it must mean hard, complicated, and impossible to understand," said Doon.

"So what about the rest of the pages?"

"Three of them have charts and graphs and diagrams that I can't make any sense of at all," said Doon. "The other four are torn and smudged, but I can more or less read them. I went through and underlined things that seemed like clues. I'll show you, later on."

"But are they *useful* clues?" Lina asked. "Do they tell us what we're looking for? And where it might be?"

Doon looked off into the distance with a slight frown. "Well, sort of," he said. "I mean, yes, definitely, *some* of them are useful, I'm sure."

Lina listened with dismay. "You mean," she said, "that we really don't know much more than we did three days ago?"

"We know a *little* more," said Doon.

"But we're going on this trip anyhow?"

Doon stopped walking then and turned to her with a sort of half smile. "Do you wish we hadn't come?"

Lina realized she didn't really wish that. A feeling of uneasiness lurked at the back of her mind, and what Doon had just said about the book made it worse. But still, it was glorious to be out here, on their own, hiking across the hills in pursuit of a mystery—even if the mystery was never solved. "No," she said, smiling back. "I'm glad we came."

When the sun told them it was around noon, they stopped to eat the first of the food they'd brought, and then, without resting long, went on their way again. Far up in the sky, toward the east, great black-winged birds floated in soundless circles.

"Do you see them?" Lina said, pointing. "Kenny said they come after the wolves have killed something."

Doon gazed up, shading his eyes. "I suppose they come when anything dies, whether wolves have killed it or not."

Lina nodded, thinking about this. It seemed horrible to her, the way animals killed each other, the pain and blood and gruesome death. She could not understand why this world, which was so full of beauty and wonder, had to also be so full of horrors.

"Doon," she said. "I just thought of something. There might be—I mean, not everyone got out of

Ember. We might find . . . we might come across—" She stopped and swallowed. "There couldn't be anyone still alive there, could there?"

"I doubt it," said Doon. "How could they find food in total darkness? And if the generator has stopped, there wouldn't be water pumped up into the city."

"Then there might be dead people."

"I know," Doon said. "I thought about that, too. It would be awful. But we have to be ready for it."

After that, they walked in silence again for a while, both occupied with somber thoughts. This would not be the lively, familiar city of their memories; they knew that. It would be a dead city, and there might be dead bodies in it. They would need all their courage.

They came to the top of another ridge of hills from which they could see a great expanse of land. "The world is absolutely *huge,*" said Lina.

"Yes, and what we can see is only a tiny, tiny bit of it." Doon told Lina about a map Edward had shown him in a book. Edward (who had learned this from the town schoolteacher) had explained that Sparks was no more than a minute dot in the big pink area that stood for the whole land, which was only one of the lands in the unimaginably enormous world. "There were words all over the map," Doon said. "They were the names of cities and towns that used to be everywhere, before the Disaster."

"Did you know," said Lina, "that some people in

faraway places speak in other languages, with completely different words from ours? Doctor Hester told me that."

"I know it," Doon said. "A few books in the Ark have other languages in them."

"It's so strange, isn't it?" Lina said. "Why would you use all different words instead of the ones everyone already knows?"

"I'm not sure," said Doon. "So much is mysterious here."

They walked on and on. Lina's feet hurt where her shoes rubbed against her heels. Doon stopped now and then to stare at something that interested him—once it was a lizard sunbathing on a rock, another time a huge black and yellow beetle. "Just *look* at it!" Doon said, picking up the beetle and letting it crawl on his hand. "It's gorgeous! Who could ever think up such a thing?" Lina would just as soon have skipped the lizards and beetles and moved on a little faster. A sharp wind started up, and she pulled her cap farther down over her ears. It seemed to her they'd gone a tremendous distance, and still their goal wasn't in sight. The daylight would be fading soon. She felt a nip of fear.

But a little later, they came to the stream that the refugees from Ember had followed on their first trip, and the broken, weedy road that ran beside it. Then they knew for sure they were on the right track. They circled around the base of a great rock that thrust up out of the ground like a giant's shoulder, rising in rounded humps higher than they were tall. "I think I remember seeing this rock when we came out of Ember," Lina said. "After we'd been walking only a little while."

Doon thought he remembered it, too. "We should be there soon," he said.

The sun sank lower in the sky, and the gray twilight settled down. Night was coming. Lina thought of the warm kitchen at home and shivered.

Ten or fifteen minutes later, they came to a place they instantly recognized.

"There it is!" Lina cried. She put down her pack and ran forward, up the slope, with Doon right behind her. It was the strangest feeling, to be here again, to see that opening in the mountainside that had been their gateway to a new world. It looked the same, a dark hole in the rock big enough for a wide wagon to go through.

They peered inside. Had anyone been here since that day they came out from Ember? If so, there was no sign of it. Maybe a wanderer took shelter in here now and then from the rain; maybe an animal slept here sometimes. But all they saw was the empty cave and the path leading inward and down.

"Think if we'd come out in the winter instead of in the summer," Lina said. "We might not have seen the moon or the stars, if it had been a cloudy night. And the grass wouldn't have been green, and we'd have been cold."

"And even if we'd seen the fox," Doon said, "he wouldn't have had that plum in his mouth, and so we wouldn't have known to eat the plums ourselves."

They stood there at the cave's edge for a bit, thinking about how lucky they'd been. Then Doon shouldered his pack again, and Lina went back and fetched hers.

"Now," he said, "the next thing is to go up and around, that way"—he pointed—"and find that little crack where we went in."

It wasn't hard to find. The first time, it had taken ages, because they hadn't known what they were looking for. This time they went almost straight to it: a spot where a low place in the ground, a sort of dent, led to a narrow slit in the mountainside.

The sun was sitting just at the horizon now; in a few minutes, darkness would fall.

"We'll just go in and look," Doon said. "And then we'll make our camp for the night."

They pulled candles from their packs and lit them. Then they edged into the passage and slowly, taking small steps, made their way along its twists and turns. Their shadows loomed beside them on the rocky walls, and the passage had the dank smell of old, cold dirt.

"Almost there, I think," said Lina, who was in front. "Yes—here's the edge."

Just ahead, the light of her candle showed the edge where the ground dropped away. She reached back for

Doon's hand, and he came up beside her. This was where they'd stood when they threw the message down to their dying city—the message that saved Ember's people. Lina remembered exactly how it had felt to fling that bundle—the scrap of paper wrapped in Doon's shirt and weighted with a rock—as hard and as far as she could. Then, they'd been able to see the lights of Ember far below. Now, of course, there was only a vast darkness.

"Wait," said Doon. "I think—"

"Me too," said Lina. "It looks like—"

Doon lowered his voice to a whisper. "Let's blow out our candles, just for a moment."

They did. They gazed downward. It was unmistakable. A dim, pulsing orange light shone from somewhere in the heart of the city.

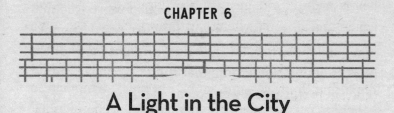

CHAPTER 6

A Light in the City

They stood there a long time, staring, then blinking and staring again to make sure their eyes weren't playing tricks on them. With their candles out, the darkness was complete except for that distant light. They couldn't even see each other's faces. But the more they looked, the more sure they were: a light shone in Ember.

"Someone is still down there," Doon breathed.

"Or maybe not," Lina said. "Maybe there's a tiny bit of electricity left. Maybe it's just a streetlamp still glowing."

They stared for a few minutes longer, wondering. Doon knelt carefully and stretched a hand over the edge of the cliff. "It seems to go straight down," he said. "But I can't really tell."

"It's a long way down," said Lina. "I don't see how we can possibly get there."

"We *have* to," said Doon. "Now that we've seen that light, we have to know what it is." Lina heard him take in a quick breath. "Oh!" he said. "It might be what the book is about! Something that shines! We have to find out. There must be a way down."

"Tomorrow we'll look for it," Lina said. A whole day of walking had tired her out, and she knew Doon was tired, too, though he might not want to admit it.

They went back through the passage and out into the waning evening light. Their shadows stretched like long fingers across the ground. Stars were beginning to come out, and both Lina and Doon gazed upward at them. They still marveled, having grown up under the black, unchanging sky of Ember, at a sky full of lights.

"Look at that one," Lina said, pointing. One star, bigger than the rest, was moving at a slow, steady pace. Its light was greenish rather than white.

"A traveling star," said Doon. "It must be what that roamer was talking about. Edward has a book about stars. I'll look up traveling stars when we get back."

They made their way around the mountainside to the place where the dark cave opening loomed in the mountain wall. Inside the cave, toward the rear, the ground was more or less dry. They spread their blankets. It was a gloomy place—dampness seeped from the walls, and Lina could feel the cold breath of the tunnel that stretched away behind them, leading down deep into the earth to the underground river they'd ridden out of Ember. But Doon was scraping out a shallow pit in the dirt to build a fire in; that would help. "I'll look for kindling," Lina said. She reached into her pack for a match to relight her candle, because full darkness had arrived by now. But Doon stopped her.

"Here," he said. "Take this. We need to save candles and matches whenever we can." From his pack, he took the little generator he had made at the end of summer from a magnet, some wires, and a crank. He'd attached a socket to it, one he'd taken from an old light fixture in the Pioneer Hotel, and screwed a light bulb into it. "You'll have to keep turning the crank," he said, handing it to her. "But it will give you more light than a candle."

Lina grinned. She'd almost forgotten about the generator, having seen it working only once. She turned the handle, and the light bulb glowed, and the cave became a bright little hollow, almost cozy. "Wonderful," she said. She set down the generator and tied her sack to her belt so she'd have both hands free, and she went out into the darkness, heading for a grove of trees to the left of the cave entrance, cranking the little generator as she went. It gave her enough light to see the ground a few feet ahead of her. When she stepped in among the trees, it helped her to see where twigs lay in the leaf litter and to avoid stumbling into prickly shrubs and tripping on the rough ground. Each time she found sticks that looked dry enough for kindling, she stopped cranking, picked the sticks up, and thrust them in her sack. The light dimmed as the crank slowed, but if she was quick, it didn't quite go out.

Finding dry sticks wasn't easy; most of them were in among the sodden leaves that covered the ground. She decided that the best way was to break small dead branches from the trees. She went deeper into the grove, looking behind to make sure she didn't lose track of the way out. Once she stopped, startled, thinking she'd seen her light reflect off something ahead of her. An animal's eye? She thought of wolves. Someone had told her they had yellow eyes. Did wolves lurk in the woods, waiting to pounce on people? She stood still for a moment, listening. She heard no sound, but just in case something was there, she decided to turn around and get out of the woods. She had enough kindling anyhow. She hurried back to the camp.

"I saw something shiny in there," she said to Doon. "Would a wolf's eye reflect light?"

"I suppose so," Doon said. "But lots of other things would, too. A piece of metal. An old glass bottle or something."

"I guess it wasn't a wolf," said Lina, setting down her bag of kindling, "because it didn't make a sound or move. Or try to eat me."

They set to work to build their fire. They put it near the mouth of the cave so the smoke could escape, and by its dancing flames, they ate their skimpy dinner. The night was silent except for the crackle of the fire—

until, far away, they heard a faint, high cry, and then more cries, weaving together into a fierce song.

"Night birds?" said Doon.

"No, I think it's wolves," Lina said. "Kenny told me they sing."

They listened, but the cries quickly died away.

"That reminds me," said Doon. "Let me show you something Kenny taught me." He went outside the cave, plucked a sturdy grass blade from the ground, and clamped it between the sides of his thumbs. Then he blew hard against it, and an amazingly loud noise, part squawk and part shriek, blasted out into the air. Lina jumped and then laughed. "How did you *do* that?"

Doon showed her how it worked. "It's a wolf-scaring whistle, Kenny told me. All you need is one blade of grass."

They practiced making whistles and earsplitting noises for a while. Then, by the light of the little generator, Doon read Lina the clues he'd picked out from the remains of the eight-page book.

"Here on page sixty-one," he said, "is something about distance. " 'More than ninety million miles,' it says. I'm not sure how long a mile is."

"But ninety million of them sounds like a long way, even if a mile is short," said Lina. "I hope it doesn't mean we have to walk for ninety million miles."

"On the same page," Doon said, "there's something about a square yard. That could be a space that's a yard long on each side—or it could be a backyard that's a square shape. 'Square yard receives,' it says. Then there's a smudge, and the only two words I can read in the rest of the sentence are 'jewel' and 'second.'"

Lina peered over his shoulder. "But they've spelled 'jewel' wrong," she said. "It isn't j-o-u-l-e."

"It's an ancient document," Doon said. "They probably spelled things differently in those days." Doon squinted at the smudged page in the unsteady light. "And then on page sixty-five," he went on, "there's part of a sentence that says, 'those which are positive and those which are negative . . .' And then, '. . . lose, gain, or share them, which creates . . .' So that could mean something about having a positive or negative view of things, or about sharing . . ." He trailed off.

"Maybe," said Lina. "Not too helpful, though."

"But then listen to this," Doon said, turning to the next page, which was half torn away. "Here it says, '. . . a number of cells of many sizes and shapes, connected . . .'" He looked up at Lina triumphantly. "What does that remind you of?"

"A cell is a room, isn't it?" she said. "Like a cell in the Ember prison. So rooms connected to each other—it sounds like the storerooms."

"Yes!" Doon said. "I think it could be."

"All right," Lina said. "Well, at least we have a little bit to go on." She felt only slightly encouraged, though. Had they come up here to find a jewel in someone's yard? Or to spend endless hours searching for a jewel in the storerooms? She had never cared much for jewels. In Ember, a jewel had been anything a person used as decoration for the body. Some people had worn bits of polished glass on strings around their necks, or bracelets of shiny metal. In Sparks, she had seen jewels sometimes on the harnesses of oxen, and now and then a roamer would bring something called jewelry from the ancient world, just some pretty stones wired together. No one got very excited about it. But she supposed they might be useful for trading.

It was time to sleep. The night was long and cold, and the ground was hard. But no animals or people disturbed them, and at the first light of morning, they were up and readying themselves to investigate the way into Ember.

Once again they stood on the ledge, looking down. The light they'd seen the night before was still there, dim but distinct.

"It's a strange sort of light," said Doon. "I think it *must* have something to do with what the book was about. Someone else has found it, whatever it was."

"Maybe," said Lina. "But then why would they stay in Ember with it? Why not bring it out?"

"Because they're trapped," Doon said. In his voice was a rising excitement. "Somehow, they didn't hear about the way out." He had brought his generator into the cave with him; he handed it to Lina. "Would you crank this?" he asked. "I want to try and see how steep the cliff is." Lina had brought a candle with her in case one was needed; she put it in her back pocket, where it wobbled, being too tall to fit all the way in.

Carefully, Doon lowered himself to his knees and then lay down completely so that his head was just over the edge of the cliff. Lina stretched out both hands as far as she dared, one holding the generator and the other cranking, and Doon peered down. He'd been hoping the slope was more gentle than it had seemed, making it possible to walk or perhaps slide down. Or maybe steps had been cut into it long ago by the Builders of Ember. Or perhaps they'd left a ladder of some kind. But as far as he could tell, the cliff was bare, vertical rock. The only way to descend from here into the city would be to have a very long rope and climb down it—or many long ropes tied together, the distance was so great. The rope would have to be anchored to something at the top—maybe a sturdy spike driven into the ground. It might be possible to rig up a pulley system for hoisting things from below. But it would all be difficult.

Doon sighed and got to his feet again. "I don't know," he said. "I'm not sure how we can do it. It would be really hard to get down there. And even harder to get back up."

"I wish we could fly down," Lina said.

They stood for a few more minutes. Lina stopped

cranking the generator, and they stared down at the one dim, wavering light still shining in their old home. Then Doon turned around to head back into the passage to the outside. As Lina turned to follow him, the candle sticking up from her back pocket struck the cave wall and toppled out. Oh, no, she thought. She assumed the candle had fallen over the edge of the cliff—but when she started up the generator again and looked down, she saw the candle not far from her feet. It was rolling very slowly away, not out toward the edge but sideways.

She took a step toward it, moving along the ledge with her back to the cave wall. The candle rolled a little farther. She took another step—and she saw that the ledge continued. It was not just a short shelf jutting out at the end of the passage. It extended to the side, on the left, making a narrow path, with the cave wall on one side and the steep drop on the other. She couldn't see very far ahead with her one light bulb. But it looked as if the path sloped downward. It might wind along the wall all the way to the bottom.

She let go of the generator's crank long enough to stoop quickly and pick up the candle. Then she turned around and hurried through the passage to the outside, where Doon was starting along the mountainside. "There's a path," she said breathlessly. "Going down."

It was a steep path, and rough, and narrow. They followed it with extreme caution, one slow step after another, keeping one hand on the wall beside them. They lit their way with candles; this was no place to have both hands occupied with the generator. At first, their idea had been to go just a little way, to see if the path continued. After they'd been walking for several minutes, it seemed that the path really might take them down to the level of the city.

"This is going to work," said Doon. "I'm sure it is. We have to go back up and get our packs."

They did so. They took out everything that wasn't essential, leaving in mainly candles and matches. They'd each brought ten matches on the trip and had used two of Lina's so far. Doon included his generator. Lina added some pieces of paper and a pencil stub that Doon's father had found and given to her, because you never knew when you might have to draw something or write a note. Each of them took one of the clever leather water bottles made in Sparks, with a plug and a strap for hooking to a belt. They rolled the rest of their supplies into the blankets they'd brought and hid the blanket rolls between some rocks. Then once again, each of them holding a candle, they went through the narrow passage and started down the path.

It was far from easy. They couldn't tell if the path had been constructed by people or if it was just a natural ledge along the wall of the cave. In some places it was partly crumbled away, and they had to step across gaps. Other places were blocked by rockslides that they had to scramble over. Always, though they couldn't see it, they were aware of the long drop into darkness just inches from their feet. But frightening as it was, they weren't willing to turn around, because the path led steadily down.

It went by way of switchbacks—they'd walk a long way in one direction, and then the path would make a tight turn and they'd find themselves walking the other way. Lina imagined how the path would look to someone gazing up at it from below—a great zigzag sweeping back and forth across the wall of the cave. Maybe someone was down there now, watching their two dots of light slowly descending.

Little by little, the smudge of light far below in the city grew closer. They stopped every now and then to check, shielding the candlelight with their hands so they could see into the depths. After about an hour, they had to stop to light new candles. They knew an hour had passed, because Doon had figured out, before they left, how long it took one candle to burn down to a stub so that they could use candles a bit like clocks—two inches gone, that meant the candle had been burning for about fifteen minutes. Each candle was about eight inches long and burned for about an hour. The candles they were carrying were now too short to hold. They stopped to get new ones from their packs and went on, step after cautious step, steadily downward.

Then Doon, who was ahead, gave a startled cry. "Here's the end!" he said. "I'm at the bottom."

Lina came up behind him, and they stood side by side with their candles showing them each other's faces, shadowy and orange. When they looked down, they saw bare ground, uneven, strewn with small rocks and pebbles.

"Can you believe it?" said Doon. "We're in the Unknown Regions."

"And going to Ember," said Lina. "There it is."

Across the ocean of darkness, she could see a faint and wavering glow. They began making their way toward it.

CHAPTER 7

Calamity

They walked slowly, keeping close together, looking carefully before each step in case the sudden deep pits or nightmarish beasts that people had always whispered about were really there. Doon was using the generator now, cranking it briskly. Lina, walking right beside him, held a candle. Their circle of light was bigger than with the candles alone. But all they saw in it was sandy-colored ground scattered with rocks and pebbles, with an occasional crack or ridge that they had to step over.

"There's litter out here," Lina said after a while. She pointed with her foot at an empty can. A few steps farther on, there was another empty can, and not far beyond that, a broken jar. "How did this stuff get here?"

"Rats, I guess," said Doon. "They must have dragged it out from the Trash Heaps."

Since they were now on the same level as the city instead of looking down into it from above, they didn't see the light as a spot anymore but as a dim background glow that made a few edges and corners of buildings visible. And they could see this glow only when they paused now and then and Doon stopped cranking his generator, because the brightness of the generator's light bulb blinded them to the fainter light beyond. It was lucky, Lina thought, that there was light in the city at all. If the darkness had been complete, they wouldn't even have known where the city was; they could have wandered around in the Unknown Regions for a long time before heading in the right direction, and they wouldn't have known it was the right direction until they'd practically bumped into a building.

Step by step, they moved on, lighting their way just a few feet ahead, and suddenly the lit ground in front of their feet disappeared into darkness.

Baffled at first, they came to a halt. Then Doon crept forward, inches at a time. Lina heard him gasp and say, "Oh, no."

"What?"

"The ground ends," Doon said. "It drops away here. We're standing on the edge of . . . I don't know, a hole or a chasm."

Lina stepped forward and stood beside him and

looked down. The toes of their shoes were right up against a black emptiness. She couldn't tell how deep or wide it was; their light penetrated only a few feet down and forward, and beyond that all was dark.

"We'll have to go around it," Doon said. "We can't go down in there."

"Never," said Lina with a shudder.

"Let's try going to the left," said Doon.

They backed away from the edge, turned, and with great caution headed along the rim of the hole. Minutes passed, and more minutes, and still they were walking beside the black emptiness, on and on.

"It isn't a hole, then," said Doon finally. "It's a sort of ditch." He pondered for a moment. "It might go all the way around the city."

"A ring," Lina said. "To keep people from leaving."

This brought them to a stop. Lina recalled the whispered rumors she'd heard all her life—about people who had gone out into the Unknown Regions and never returned. They could be down there— what was left of them.

"We have to go back," she said. "We can't get across it."

"I wish we could tell how wide it is," said Doon. "If it's deep but not very wide, then maybe we could."

"How?" said Lina. "Jump?" She meant this as a joke, but Doon didn't laugh.

He said, "Didn't you bring some scraps of paper with you?"

"Yes."

"Can I have a couple of them?" Doon asked. "I have an idea."

Lina pulled two of her scraps of paper from her pack and handed them to him. Doon bent over and looked around until he found a small stone on the ground. He wrapped the stone in the paper and held the paper to Lina's candle until it caught fire, and then quickly he threw the flaming packet out over the chasm. It flew up and then dropped, farther and farther, until it struck with a small tap far below their feet and went out.

"One more try," said Doon. "I'll throw harder."

He lit the little packet and heaved it with all his strength. This time it flew out in a long arc and landed at the same level as the ground they were standing on. It looked to Lina to be maybe ten feet away. "So it's a deep crevice," Doon said. "But not all that wide."

"Too wide to get across," said Lina. "We have to turn around."

So they retraced their steps. The chasm now yawned on their other side. Lina forced fearsome pictures from her mind: rats crawling up over the edge, other creatures even worse than rats. . . . "Let's hurry," she said.

They came to the place where they'd begun, recognizing it by the bits of litter that lay on the ground there. "This is where we go back to the path," said Doon. "But I hate to give up, now that we've come all this way."

"We have to," Lina said. "Otherwise we'll just walk around and around and never get to the city."

"We don't know that for sure. Let's go a little farther, just in case."

And after only a few steps, they saw the way. Two thick planks stretched across the chasm. "Someone made a bridge," Doon said.

It was not a bridge that inspired confidence. Narrow, slightly sagging, with no rails to hold on to, it reached out into the darkness, and below waited the invisible depths. But beyond was the city.

"Shall we try?" asked Doon.

Lina just nodded, not trusting herself to speak.

Doon put his generator back in his pack and lit a candle from the flame of Lina's. Then he started across. With each step, he paused, looking ahead and not down. The planks creaked beneath his feet. Lina held her breath, as if even breathing too hard might knock Doon off balance. His light drew farther away, but quite soon he turned to face her from the other side. "You can do it!" he cried. "It's not hard!"

She stepped out. She looked only at her feet—one step, and then the next. The boards of the bridge shuddered a little beneath her. It was good, she thought, that she couldn't see how deep the space below her was. She was almost there. Doon stood just ahead. She would have been fine if she had not let her eyes stray at the last moment and caught a glimpse of white. In spite of herself, she turned to see: a tumble of pale sticks on the slope of the pit, just below her. Bones.

She staggered and fell to her knees. Her candle dropped into the pit and went out. She clung there, gripping the boards with her hands.

"Don't move!" cried Doon. "I'm coming!"

She waited, all her muscles clenched, and in a moment Doon was in front of her. She gripped his hand, stood up, and followed him on shaky legs to the bridge's end.

"All right?" he said.

She nodded, but her mind was spinning. She knew people died. She knew that the dead of Ember were carried out past the Trash Heaps, that the Song of Goodbye was sung for them, and that their bodies were left for the rats and worms to deal with. Everyone in Ember knew this. But to think about those who had fallen to their deaths alone in the darkness, in terror—that was different. "Let's go," she said. "I want to get away from here."

So they hurried on, lighting the way with just Doon's candle, now that the haze of light from the city was so close.

"Do you smell something?" Lina asked.

Doon sniffed. "I do. Smells like smoke."

"Could a building be on fire?" Lina wondered.

"I don't know," said Doon. "I hope not."

They walked on. The orange light stayed more or less steady, though the smell of smoke grew stronger.

They realized they had reached the city when a wall suddenly appeared not five feet in front of them. The candlelight, instead of making a circle beneath their feet, seemed to fold upward at the farthest edge. A few steps closer, and they could put their hands out and feel the chilly stone of the building. Doon raised his candle higher to see if there were any clues about what building they had come to—but of course there weren't. None of the buildings in Ember had windows or doors on the side that faced the Unknown Regions.

Keeping one hand on the wall, they made their way along until they came to a corner, and there Lina looked for a street sign. She found it easily—a pole with its small printed rectangle on top. "Deeple Street," she said, and in her mind, the whole city and their position in it fell into place. "We're on the north side—in Farwater Square. Look, here's a light pole." Doon's candle lit up the base of the pole, but the top, where before a great lamp would have been shining, was lost in darkness. On the corner of Deeple and Blott streets, an old white rocking chair stood, for some reason. Maybe someone had put it out as trash, although to Lina it looked perfectly sturdy.

"All right, good," said Doon. "So first let's find where that light is coming from." Lina took out a candle and lit it from Doon's. She wanted to see everything as well as possible.

They started down Blott Street, Doon ahead and Lina close behind. It was strange and thrilling to be in her old city. Even though their candles lit only a very small area around them, her memory easily filled in the rest. Here was one of Ember's many old-clothes shops, the one run by Sarmon Grole. Here was the market where she'd bought so many turnips and beets and jars of baby food. Here was the house where she'd once taken a message to an old man who collected string. It was all familiar, but so strange, too, because of the silence and emptiness. No people bustled past the stone buildings anymore; the great streetlamps fixed to the buildings' eaves no longer sent out yellow pools of light. Lina's candlelight glimmered on dark, cracked shop windows, fell into the gulf of open doors, and lit bottom steps of stairways, where sometimes there was a sock or a scarf, dropped by someone in a hurry to leave. Lina peered at everything she passed, identifying, remembering.

By the time they came to Cloving Square, she'd fallen quite a distance behind Doon. She saw that he, too, must be absorbed in remembering, because he didn't seem to notice she was no longer near him. She hurried to catch up; they mustn't get separated. But she couldn't help pausing once again when she came to the messengers' station.

This was where she'd come on the first day of her first job, which had been assigned to her on her last day of school. She'd been given her red jacket and told the rules, and then she'd been off—running through the streets of the city, carrying messages everywhere. She'd loved being a messenger. She gazed at the empty spot, where beside a door was a bench with a couple of red jackets flung across it.

A wave of sadness washed over her, and she looked away and hurried on up the street toward the tiny glow of Doon's candle far ahead.

Then suddenly she heard a shout. Doon's voice— what was he saying? She froze, trying to hear. Another shout: "No! No!" and with it, voices that were not Doon's. So people were here after all. But what Lina was hearing didn't sound like friendly greetings.

She started to run—but she went too fast. Before

she'd gone ten steps, the air rushing past blew her candle out.

There was nothing to do but stop. She stood where she was (on Greystone Street, almost, she thought, to Passwall), peered at the glimmerings in the distance that now looked like two candles, not just one, and listened. The gruff voices growled and snarled and overlapped each other, and she couldn't make out the words, but Doon's voice rose high and clear. "Let go of me!" he cried.

Terror drained away Lina's strength. But she knew when she saw the lights fade and the voices grow more distant that she had to move. She had to keep track of Doon; she couldn't lose him. She would have to run, and without her candle, the only light came from way up ahead of her, from the people who'd caught Doon and the dim glow behind them. Quickly she bent down, took her shoes off, and thrust them into her backpack. She could go more quietly in her socks. Then, keeping her eyes on the tiny lights ahead and one hand stretched out, fingers brushing the wall, she ran.

Doon's voice came again. "I *did* come alone! I'm *by myself*!"

Lina understood. *Do not let them see you.* That was Doon's message. Someone had caught him, and she musn't let it happen to her.

She traced the map of Ember in her mind as she went. I'm behind the Gathering Hall now. I'm passing Roving Street, on my right. She hardly let herself breathe, for fear she might be heard. She ran as fast as she could without being able to see where she was stepping, and very soon she drew close to the voices and the moving lights. Too close. She couldn't just run up behind them and follow along. She would have to get ahead of them somehow, find a hiding place she could watch from, and see who they were and what they were doing with Doon.

So she turned and went along the back of the Gathering Hall. If she went fast, she could hide behind the trash bin at the far corner by the Prison Room and see if they came out into Harken Square or went another way. There was the chance that she'd get confused—complete darkness can erase your mental map, as she well knew. But if she was sure she was out of sight, she could light her candle again. So she crept forward, rounded the corner of the Gathering Hall, and placed herself behind the trash bin. The light here was brighter than ever, and the smoke smell was stronger.

Now that she had stopped running, Lina found that she was shaking all over. Everything had happened so suddenly. Their plan, which had been going so well, had been changed in an instant. Now what? *Now* what?

As if in answer to her question, Doon's voice pierced the darkness again. He was farther away now. His words weren't as clear. But what she thought she heard was, "Get away! Go home! Get—" There was a pause, and then "Help!" Was this a message meant for her? Was he telling her to go home and get help? She wasn't sure.

Cautiously, moving a fraction of an inch at a time, she looked out from behind the trash bin. Right away, she saw them: two men with Doon between them, on the far side of Harken Square, each with a grip on one of Doon's arms. And in the center of the square, so bright it made her squint, was the source of the orange light they'd seen from above. It was indeed a fire.

Lina had gotten past the terror of open flames that she'd had when she first arrived in Sparks. She'd become used to fire, at least the kind of fire that's helpful, the kind that lets you cook and keep warm. But this was a big, disorderly fire, right on the pavement, a spreading heap of charred rubble, shooting up flames in some spots and smoldering in others. It cast a wavering orange glare out across Harken Square, on the kiosks where old posters still hung, on the wide steps of the Gathering Hall—and on three figures who scurried around the fire's edges: one big one and two smaller ones.

As Lina watched, the tallest of the fire-tenders bent over, picked something up in one hand, and threw it toward the fire. Lina saw its black silhouette as it fell, flapping and fluttering, toward the flames. Sheets of paper, she thought. In fact, she was sure—it was a book.

CHAPTER 8

Prisoner

Later on, Doon would be grateful for two things about that awful moment when the men appeared. One was that Lina had lagged behind, so only he was captured. And the other was that the straps of his pack had been pressing painfully on his shoulders just before it happened, so he'd taken the pack off to readjust it. When he saw the two men, he was so startled that he let it fall.

He had just passed the corner of Roving Street, and there they suddenly were ahead of him, first one, then the other, two dark shapes emerging from a doorway, each with a light, and each one carrying some sort of bag or bundle.

His immediate impulse was to greet them. He stepped forward and called out, and they whirled around at the sound of his voice. Doon saw that somehow they wore their lights on their heads. He saw that one was short and stocky and the other slightly taller and thin, but aside from that, he couldn't see them well enough to tell if they were people he knew.

"Hello!" he said, moving toward them. "Who are you?"

They stood silent. Doon stared, trying to get a look at their faces. Why weren't they answering? Then one of them muttered something to the other, and they dropped their bags and sprang at him. Doon backed away, stumbling, trying to turn, but he didn't move quickly enough. His right arm was grabbed, then his left, and though he twisted and pulled, he found himself caught fast. He shouted, "No! No!" His candle fell to the pavement and went out.

He still could see nothing of the people who'd grabbed him—they were just shaggy dark hulks with a bad smell and lights that seemed to be growing out of their foreheads. Their hands circled his upper arms like bands of steel. The person on his left spoke. "The question is," he said, "not who are we, but who are *you*? *You're* the trespasser."

Doon tried again to pull away. "Let go of me!" he cried. But the two men were strong, though they were hardly taller than he was.

"Don't struggle," said the one on his right, "or we'll twist your arms off."

"Yorick, you muttonhead, shut your mouth," said the one on the left. "We're not twisting off any arms. Just march him this way and be quiet."

Doon knew at once that these were not people of Ember. Though he hadn't known every single citizen of his old city, he knew there was no one who sounded like these two. Or had lights like theirs, either. Now that they were right next to him, he saw that each of them wore a kind of lantern—a cap with a tube attached at the front, and in the tube a candle, like a glowing horn. The candles cast weird, downward-pointing shadows on their faces, but Doon could tell that the shorter man was older and hairier than the taller one, and the taller one had either a small mustache or a shadow beneath his nose.

Doon's mind went in crazy zigzags as they dragged him along. He opened his mouth to call for help from Lina, and then snapped it closed again. No, he couldn't let them know she was here. She could help him only if she wasn't a prisoner, too.

"This is our place, boy," said the man on his left, the older one. "We run it. No intruders allowed, and no sightseers. You're going to have to explain yourself."

"Somebody musta come with him, Pa," said the one on his right, who had a high, whiny voice. "A kid wouldn't come down in such a place alone." He gave Doon's arm a vicious squeeze.

Doon yelped.

"Don't hurt him, Yorick, you brainless bucket," said the one called Pa. "We can use him. Don't want him crippled." He tugged Doon's other arm. "So who came with you, boy? We know you didn't come alone."

"I *did* come alone! I'm *by myself*!" Doon shouted it at the top of his voice, hoping Lina could hear him and wouldn't come flying to his rescue. Stay hidden, he thought at her. Help me, but don't let them see you.

"No need to yell," said the older man. "We're not deaf."

But Doon was desperate to let Lina know that she mustn't come after him. She wouldn't be strong enough to get him free; they'd only capture her, too. She needed to go back to Sparks for help. He had to tell her that somehow. He could think of only one way to do it.

They turned down Otterwill Street. Doon threw himself into a frenzy of yanking and pulling and wrenching, at the same time yelling up a storm. "GET AWAY from me," he cried out, making the first two words much louder than the second two. "I want to GO HOME! GET your hands off me. HELP!" What Lina would hear—he hoped—was "GET AWAY! GO HOME! GET HELP!" It was the best he could do.

He stopped struggling. The two men gripped him more tightly than ever. "No use throwing a fit," said the older one. "You'll just get yourself all worn out and banged up."

They turned into Harken Square. Doon gaped. Here he was in one of the places most familiar to him in the world, and it was utterly, horribly changed.

The light they'd seen from above clearly had nothing to do with the eight-page book. It was simply a fire, burning right in the middle of the square, sending out a haze of smoke. In one place a sort of living room had been set up, with a table and some armchairs and a few carpets. There was a washtub full of water, and empty cans and jars cluttered the ground. Around this living area were heaps of bags and stacks of boxes, in some of which Doon could see familiar-looking jars—he recognized pickled beets, powdered potatoes, and dried purple beans. So there was at least some food left here, maybe even more than he'd thought. Three people moved around the fire's edges.

In the light of the fire, Doon could finally get a better look at his captors. The older one, on his left, was built like a stack of bricks—wide in the shoulders, stout in the chest, a thick neck, and a head that looked too big for his body. He had an immense amount of rust-colored hair—it sprang wildly from beneath the candle-cap on his head, it covered the entire lower half of his face in a tangled thicket of mustache and beard, and it poked out of his ears and his nostrils. His eyebrows were like the eaves of a thatched roof overhanging his eyes.

The younger one was taller and thinner, with little anxious-looking eyes that darted this way and that. He did have a small mustache, and on his chin was a brownish scruff of hairs, a feeble attempt at a beard. From both these people came a strong smell, a smell of clothes unwashed for a long time, a grubby, sweaty smell.

"Look what we found!" cried the younger one as the others came running up to them. "A trespasser!"

"I'm not a trespasser," Doon said. He tried again to wrench himself free, but the men's grip on him only tightened.

The other people came up close to him and stared. They all wore the candle-caps. One was a woman in dark clothes with black hair pulled tight against her head. She peered at him with small, mournful eyes. "Oh, trouble," she said. "Woe and alas. Daughter, come close."

A girl who looked about Doon's age came and stood beside her mother. She was wide-shouldered and rusty-haired like the older man. She squinted at Doon, grinning. In her hand was a long fork, with which she gave Doon a poke in the leg.

"Now, boy," said the man on Doon's left. "You have blundered into the domain of the Trogg family, which you see before you. Myself, Washton Trogg, known as Trogg to the world and Pa to the family. My wife, Minny. My son, Yorick, and my daughter, Kanza."

Someone else lurked behind them—a boy, Doon thought, though he couldn't tell for sure. He didn't look like a member of the Trogg family; his hair was frizzy and pale, like a handful of soap suds, and he was small and flimsy-looking and had an oddly lopsided way of standing.

"What about that one?" Doon asked, tipping his head toward the boy.

"Oh, him," said Trogg. "He's not one of ours. We brought him with us out of pity."

"Why?"

"Bandits killed his parents," Trogg said. "So we took him in. Extra hands always welcome, I say." He pointed a finger at the pale-haired boy. "You," he said. "Bring us that wooden chair!"

The boy went over to a straight chair and dragged it up to them. Doon saw that he bent awkwardly sideways, down and up, down and up, when he walked. One of his feet was twisted at an odd angle.

Trogg turned to Doon. "Now," he said. "What is your name?"

Doon didn't want to tell him. But Yorick pinched his arm when he didn't speak, so he said, "Doon."

"Doom!" said Trogg. He grinned, revealing square yellow teeth. "What a name! Your parents must have known you were headed for trouble."

"Not *Doom*," said Doon. "Doon, with an *n*."

"Oh," said Trogg. "All right, Doon. We're going to have to tie you up for now. Sit him here, Yorick." The son pushed Doon into the chair and held him there while Trogg rooted around in the heaps of stuff and came up with a long rope. A black rage filled Doon as they wound it around him, and he kicked and thrashed and tried his best to butt them with his head—but their strength was too much for him, and in minutes he was bound up like a package, tied to the chair, hands and feet completely helpless.

The wife and daughter dragged a couple of boxes up close and sat on them to stare at the curious captured creature. The son stood next to Doon, looking eager to reach out and twist an arm if necessary. The father pulled a pair of glasses from the pocket of the loose, grubby shirt he wore. He put the glasses on and squinted through them. They had heavy dark rims and made his wide face look like a brick wall with two windows in it. His hands grasped his knees, his elbows sticking out. Behind him, the fire smoked and smoldered.

"So," he said. "What I want to know is, who are you? How did you get here? And why did you come?"

The whole family leaned forward to hear Doon's answer. Even the light-haired person lurking in the background came a few steps closer. But Doon was still so flabbergasted by the astonishing presence of these strange people in his city that his mind was a whirl of confusion. He couldn't think of an answer. He stared at the faces confronting him and at the flames just behind them. It was like being in a bad dream, the kind where you're in some familiar place—your own bedroom, or your school room—that has been strangely changed so it doesn't look like itself. Worse, it doesn't *feel* like itself. That was how Harken Square felt now. Where there used to be glowing streetlamps and people crossing the wide space on their errands, there was this savage fire and this strange and terrible family.

"Speak up!" cried Trogg. "Explain yourself!"

Doon stumbled over his words. "I just . . . I just happened to . . . I'm just here by accident. I'll leave right away."

"No," said Trogg, "you will not."

"Just try it," said the son, yanking on Doon's arm. "You'll get your bones broken."

"No breaking bones!" Trogg punched the air in his son's direction. "I'm doing the talking here. Be quiet. And get me a different pair of glasses. I can't see right through these." He yanked them off.

Yorick hurried over to a box that seemed to be full of glasses. Doon heard them rattling as Yorick shuffled through them.

"Here," Yorick said, handing his father a wire-rimmed pair. Trogg put them on. They made his eyes look huge.

"Really," said Doon. "If you let go of me, I'll leave right this minute. I was planning to anyway. Why do you think I only brought one candle?" He thought with gratitude of his pack, lying in the dark back on Greystone Street where he had set it down. "I just wanted to take a look," he went on. "Sorry to intrude. I didn't know you were here. I didn't know *any* of this was here." He made a rolling motion with his head, indicating the city. "I found a crack in the mountain, and then I . . . and then there was a path, and so . . ." He trailed off. "So if you'll just untie me, I'll get out right away."

"Not possible," said Trogg. "You don't understand. Now that you're here, you have to stay."

Crouched behind the trash bin, with the stink of old garbage in her nose, gazing in horror at the transformed Harken Square, Lina had seen Doon's captors drag him out into the square. She had watched as they tied him up and showed him off to the other people. She could see—she could *feel*—Doon's fury as the bearded man scolded him and jabbed him with questions. She, too, felt angry. Who *were* these people who thought they owned the city? But her fear was stronger than her anger.

The words Doon had called out repeated themselves in her mind. *Get away! Go home, get help. Get away! Go home, get help.* She was so stunned by what had happened, she could hardly make sense of them. Go home? What could he have meant? Her thoughts went first to the home she'd had here in Ember, over on Quillium Square, with her grandmother and Poppy. But of course that was her home no more. Her home was in Sparks now, a long day's walk across the hills. Could Doon really mean she should go back there? Back out through the Unknown Regions, back across the planks that bridged the pit, back up that long, long path?

She hid behind the trash bin until her legs began to ache from holding so still. She heard everything—or almost everything. Sometimes the voices were too low or were drowned out by a burst of crackling from the fire. But she heard enough to know that these people had taken over her city and had captured Doon and did not intend to let him go.

There *must* be some way to rescue him without going back to Sparks for help. Ideas sped through her mind:

Could she make a noise and get the Troggs to run after her, giving Doon time to untie himself and escape? No, because surely they wouldn't *all* run after her. Someone would be left behind to guard the captive. Besides, how could Doon untie himself? His hands were bound.

Could she dash out there, taking them all by surprise, and untie Doon and run off with him? No, because the untying would take too long, and they'd just capture her, too.

Could she wait and watch and hope for a chance to free him some other time? But when would that be? It might take days and days. She might *never* get the chance.

There was no other way: to get help for Doon, she'd have to go back to Sparks. All that distance, and fast, and by herself.

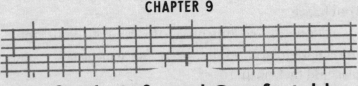

CHAPTER 9

Perfectly Safe and Comfortable

Doon stared up at Trogg's smug smile. "Stay?" he said. "What do you mean, stay?"

"I mean live here with us, of course," said Trogg. "Otherwise, you'd go out there and tell the world, right? Underground city! Room for hundreds! Pioneer family already living there, done the hard work; all we have to do is move in!"

"I wouldn't say that," said Doon.

"Of course you would. Anyone would. Then we'd have the hordes down here, ruining everything. We can't have that. This is our domain, our stronghold, our place of safety. So you'll have to stay. Don't worry, we can use you. There's plenty of work. Count yourself lucky to have found us." He scratched at his neck, digging with a grimy fingernail through the thick tangle of beard. "What were you doing, anyhow, wandering around in the mountains? Lost? Got left behind by your parents?"

Doon ignored this question. "Why do you think hordes of people would come *here*?" he said. "This place is—not fit to live in."

Trogg thrust his face toward Doon and narrowed his eyes. "Up above," he said, "life is tough. There's rain, wind, and snow, in case you haven't noticed. Food is scarce. Rats eat your grain; wolves steal your flocks. Worst of all, people are always getting in your way, bossing you around. Up there, it's work and trouble all the time."

"Oh," said Doon. He realized he'd had a similar thought himself, earlier this same day.

"Bandits, too," said Trogg. "Mustn't forget to mention bandits."

"I don't know much about bandits," Doon said.

"Well, let me tell you," said Trogg. "My family knows about them. We know a lot more than we want to know. Bandits came to our village."

The whole family pressed closer to Doon, staring down at him, their backs to the fire, their faces lit only dimly by the candles they wore in their strange caps. They were a circle of fire-horned monsters, looming over him, closing in. He stifled the urge to scream at them and struggle. It wouldn't help. He would have to use his wits to get out of this. Pay attention, pay attention, he reminded himself. It was what his father had told him when he first started working in the Pipeworks, the vast system of tunnels beneath Ember's streets, down by the river that supplied the city's water. It had helped him then. Maybe it would help him now, too. So he listened hard to what Trogg was saying.

"They came out of the forest," Trogg said, "roaring at the top of their lungs."

"They had torches," said Kanza, stretching one hand up over her head. "Three-foot-high flames."

"Oh, the terror, the terror," wailed the mother, as if she were seeing it all happening again. She clasped her head in her hands and pulled down, making her eyes droop at the sides and turning her mouth into an upside-down U. "Woe and alas! I thought our house would burn. I thought my children would die."

"And our house *did* burn!" cried Trogg. "They rampaged through the village. They set fire to our roofs; they stole the stores from our barns; they drove off our animals."

"And even worse," said Yorick, bending over to speak into Doon's ear, "they had knives and they—"

"Silence!" shouted Trogg. "I'm telling this story! They had knives as long as your arm, boy. Torch in one hand, knife in the other. Anyone stupid enough to step out of the house got sliced up like a piece of cheese."

"And not only that," said Kanza, "anyone stupid

enough to stay *inside* the house got burned up like a stick of wood!"

"Not us, though," said Yorick.

"Not us," said Trogg, "because I know trouble when I see it coming, and I hustled my family out the back just in time."

"We hid in the mud," said Kanza.

"Behind the pigsty," said Yorick.

"Oh, it was dreadful." Minny rocked from side to side, still holding her head. "The foul odors. The shrieking from beyond. But my husband is so brave, so clever, so—"

"So when those barbarian bandits had gone," Trogg interrupted, "we got busy, the few of us left in the village, treating wounds, building houses, fixing our fences and our wagons and starting all over."

"It was three years ago," said Kanza.

"No, four," said Yorick.

"Quiet!" shouted Trogg. "Your sister's right, you ignorant pup. It was three years ago. And then just a few weeks ago, I heard that more were on the way." He shook his finger in Doon's face. "Do you think I was going to sit still and wait for them to show up?"

"I don't know," said Doon, who was trying hard to pay attention to this horrible story coming at him from all directions.

"You don't know? You don't know?" screamed

Trogg. His glasses slid down his nose, and he ripped them off. "Maybe you're the kind of person who would leave his family in danger, but not me! I take action! I packed up my wagon, loaded in my family, and headed out to look for a place of safety."

"Like a remote valley," said Kanza.

"Or an ancient abandoned lodge on a high peak," said Yorick.

"But what we found," said Trogg, "was far, far better."

"It sure was," said Yorick eagerly. "You oughta see what we discovered when we went back into the—"

Trogg jumped to his feet and let loose an absolute explosion of fury and insults. When he'd finished calling Yorick a dozen kinds of mush-brained idiot, he lowered his voice and hissed at him, "We don't talk about that. Not to someone who just showed up out of nowhere. When the time comes to talk about it, *I* will do the talking."

Yorick cowered, hunching his shoulders up around his ears. "Sorry," he said. "Forgot."

"Oh, Yorick, Yorick, alas," moaned his mother. "You'll endanger us all if you aren't more careful. Listen to your father."

"To go on," said Trogg, sitting back down. "What we found was the entrance to a cave. We went in; we found a nice smooth wide path; we followed it down and down, quite a distance. And at the bottom, we found something very interesting, boy," said Trogg. "You would never guess."

I bet I would, Doon thought.

"We found a pool," said Trogg, "jammed with empty boats. *Jammed.* There must have been a hundred of 'em, just floating there, some of them wrecked, some of them half sunk. 'Something happened here,' I says to Yorick. We didn't like the look of it. We could tell these boats had come on an underground river. Only way to travel that river from where we were was to swim upstream."

"Which we didn't want to do," said Yorick.

"So we went back out, tramped around some more, and wal*lah*."

"Wal*lah*?" said Doon.

"Ancient expression," said Trogg. "It means, 'there it is.' A crack in the mountainside. And here's an interesting thing, boy, that I spotted because of my long experience observing the terrain. Somebody *made* that crack and then blocked it up."

"But it wasn't blocked," said Doon. "That's how I came in here."

"It isn't blocked *now*," Trogg said. "But it used to be. I could tell from looking at the stones lying outside it. They're covered with earth and grass now, but still, my expert eye spotted them. Too square to be natural.

What happened was, the earth shifted, and"—he put his palms together, made a growly creaking sound, and pulled them apart—"stones fell out, crack opened up," he said.

Doon was confused. "What do you mean, the earth shifted?"

Trogg goggled at him as if he were an ignoramus. "Earthquake, boy! Never heard of them? Where have you been all your life? Didn't you notice that dent in the ground leading up to the crack? It's a sure sign. Earth shakes, falls in, everything budges, things that once were closed now are open. Probably happened in that quake we had ten or twelve years ago."

"Oh," said Doon. He hadn't noticed any quake; but then, he would have been a baby, or not even born.

"So," said Trogg, "I squeezed into that crack, found a skinny passage that led to a cliff at the edge of a huge hole. And down at the bottom of that hole, I saw—"

Utter darkness, thought Doon.

"Utter darkness," said Trogg, "for a long time, and *then*—" He paused again, peering at Doon from under his bristling eyebrows—"and *then* . . . something breathing."

"What?"

"Something *breathing*, I said. Aren't you listening? It was *like* something breathing. Way down in there, a mist of light came up." Trogg put his hands low to the ground and raised them slowly. "In the light, shapes, dark shapes like buildings. And then in a couple of minutes, it went down." He floated his hands down. "Faded in, faded out. Like something breathing, like something almost dead, breathing."

"Ah," said Doon. The generator, he thought—its last gasps. Still sending out weak pulses of power now and then. He was filled with amazement and sorrow, as if the city were indeed a living thing on its way to death.

"Now," said Trogg. "I should tell you that I am a rock climber. Fearless, and skillful as a spider. I saw this place; I knew it was meant for my family. I discovered the narrow path along the wall. I went down. A solo expedition. Encountered some trouble, though. That ditch out there. Very deep."

Doon shuddered, remembering.

"Luckily," Trogg went on, "I am a person of great ingenuity. I simply tied a hammer to the rope I carried with me and hurled it across, which let me measure, more or less, the width of the thing. Not out of the question, I thought. So I jumped it."

"*What?*" said Doon, not sure if he'd heard right.

"Gave myself a good running start," said Trogg, "and then"—he chugged his arms back and forth like pistons, clenched his face into ferocious determination, and roared—"r-r-r-r-rrrrrrraaaaaargh! Ran like crazy, leaped; almost made it."

"Almost?"

"Hit the opposite bank, had to do some scrambling up through the bones and slime, but I got over." Trogg beamed, clearly proud of himself.

Doon spent a moment imagining the kind of nerve it would take to jump over that ditch in the dark. Not to mention the leg muscles. He felt a kind of horrified admiration.

Trogg went on. "I found this place. I claimed it. I named it. Darkhold, because it is the dark place where we hold off the hard and treacherous world outside." He swept out an arm in a lofty gesture, indicating his private kingdom. "Then I simply wrenched some boards off a wall, put together a decent bridge, and flopped it over the pit. Climbed back up to my family, told them my discovery. All of us came down, and we've been settling in ever since."

"How long have you been here?" Doon asked.

"Four weeks. More or less," Trogg said. "Hard to tell what divides day from night if there's no sun. But we came prepared. We've got that." He pointed, but Doon couldn't tell what he was pointing at. "The hourglass, boy!" said Trogg. "Right there, on that heap of sacks!"

Doon had never heard the word "hourglass," but he saw that it must be the thing shaped more or less like a figure eight—two glass funnel shapes attached one on top of the other, the top one right side up and the bottom one upside down, all of it held in a wooden frame. Something in the top funnel was sifting slowly down into the bottom one.

"Never seen one, hah, Droon? It works thusly: the sand trickles down from the top to the bottom in exactly eight hours. Then we turn the thing upside down, and it starts again. Sixteen hours equals day, eight hours equals night. All we have to do is remember to turn it."

"Hmm," said Doon. Actually, he thought this was a very clever device, but he didn't want to admire it out loud.

"Whoever used to live here left in a hurry," Trogg went on. "Abandoned all their stuff. This place is a treasure trove. We can live here, perfectly safe and comfortable, for a good long time. As long as no one tells the world about us." He stood up and smacked his hands together. Yorick sprang up, too, and Doon saw the light-haired person struggle to his feet. "Now," said Trogg. "We can get back to work, as soon as we take care of one thing." He raised his bristling eyebrows at Doon.

And that was when, all of a sudden, the city breathed. The streetlamps over Harken Square buzzed and sizzled and blinked. Everyone stopped moving and looked up at them. Dimly, the lamps began to shine. Faint lights showed in the upstairs windows of a few apartments. The light grew brighter and brighter, until for a moment Doon saw Ember as he remembered it, its great lamps making pools of light on the streets, casting shadows, lighting the steps and columns of the Gathering Hall. And then the lights began to fade.

But before they did, Doon's eye was caught by a quick movement down at the base of the Gathering Hall steps—a hand, fluttering. A face appeared beside it, and he realized it was Lina, leaning out from behind the big trash bin by the wall. Their eyes connected, and Doon, seeing that the Troggs were all gazing upward at the lights, shaped silent words with his mouth, hoping Lina would understand. *Go home,* he mouthed. He aimed a look upward to make clear what he meant. *Get away. Go home. Get help.* He thought he saw Lina nod—but then the lamps went out, and darkness fell again.

"So there you are," said Trogg. "That's what I was telling you about. Don't suppose you've seen anything like *that* before, have you?"

"Not exactly," said Doon.

"Think you could get used to living here?"

"No," said Doon.

"Too bad," said Trogg. "This is your new home."

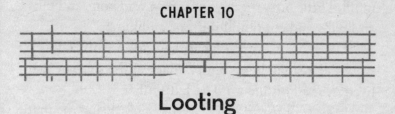

CHAPTER 10

Looting

"Now to our little problem," Trogg said. "We want you to help with our work, so you have to be able to move around. But we don't want you running off, so you ought to be tied up. But if you're tied up, you can't work. What's the solution?"

Doon said nothing.

"The solution that first occurred to me," said Trogg, "is to tie up your feet and leave your hands free. But then I thought, Trogg, that won't work. If his hands are free, he could just bend down and untie his feet. That was when I remembered some useful things we found the other day at a very interesting store. Where was that place, Yorick?"

"Over that way," said Yorick, who had flopped down into a fat, shabby armchair. He waved in the direction of Greengate Square. "Funny place, full of a million little bitty things, like screws and bolts and pins and nails and cords and buttons and knobs."

Doon went rigid. That had to be his father's store—the Small Items Shop. That was the shop he had lived over all his life until he left Ember.

"Yes, very useful place," Trogg said. "Bring me that sack, Yorick. That one, over there."

Yorick heaved himself out of the chair and fetched the sack, and Trogg dumped it out on the ground. All kinds of metal doodads clattered out. "Let's see," said Trogg. "This might work." From the heap, he pulled a couple of C-shaped handles that might have come from cupboard doors. He pressed them together to form a ring. "Just right," he said. "Now we need two more. . . . Here they are. . . . And then some screws and bolts . . . and this piece of chain. And this nifty little padlock, complete with key! Perfect. Help me here, Yorick."

Doon's heart was hammering. Shackled by a chain from his own father's store? "No," he said. As hard as he could, he rocked the chair he was tied to from side to side, but it made no difference. Yorick held him fast and Trogg worked. First he clamped a pair of handles around one of Doon's ankles and screwed them tightly together.

"Ow," said Doon. The metal pressed against his bone. Trogg ignored him. He cuffed Doon's other ankle.

Then he looped the chain through the cuffs and connected its ends with the padlock.

"There," he said, grinning his wide grin. "It's just right. Long enough so you can walk but not run. And not possible to undo, even if your hands are free, unless you can find yourself a screwdriver, which you won't be able to do, because we will be watching you all the time, or unless you get your hands on this little key." He held up the key to the padlock. "Which you also won't be able to do, because I will hide it where sneaky fingers can't find it." Trogg untied the ropes that bound Doon. He tossed them away. Then he stood back and gazed proudly at his new worker. "You'll need one more thing," he said. "A lightcap. I'll have Minny make you one. In the meantime, just stick close to my kids." He nodded to Yorick and Kanza. "You two head out," he said, "and take him with you. Pick up our bags from where we left them, and then start on that neighborhood there." He pointed over toward the school. "I'll bring the wagon and catch up with you in a moment."

So the two younger Troggs grabbed Doon's arms, and he stumbled along with them. They headed across the square and around the end of the Gathering Hall to Greystone Street, where they picked up the bags they'd dropped when they'd captured Doon. Then they turned around and started down Otterwill Street.

The cuffs chafed Doon's ankles, but the humiliation of being a slave in his own city was far worse than the pain. He tried not to think about how impossible his predicament was. If he didn't know where the key was, how would he ever get out of here? He would have to count on Lina to bring help—and the very thought of Lina, walking alone all the way back to Sparks, made him feel so anxious and so miserably guilty that his knees nearly collapsed. It had been a terrible, terrible idea to come here. He wished he had never found that wretched eight-page book.

At the corner of School Street, Trogg caught up with them. He was hauling a wooden wagon behind him; Doon recognized it as one that used to carry garbage to Ember's Trash Heaps. Trogg poked Doon in the back. "Move along, Droon!" he said. "Work to be done."

Doon jerked his head around, furious in an instant. "My name is *Doon*!" he cried. "Not Droon, not Doom! At least call me by my right name!"

Trogg backed away, grinning, stretching forward a big hand as if to ward off a blow. "All right, all right, no need to yell," he said. "Glad to see our new boy has some spirit."

"I am *not* your boy!" Doon said. "I am my own boy."

Kanza, who had hold of Doon's right arm, sniggered. "A fighter," she said. "Isn't he cute?" She made a fake cute face at him, bunching her lips as if she was going to kiss him and squeezing his arm so tightly he could feel her fingernails through his sleeve.

Doon told himself to hold his temper. Flying into a rage would help nothing. But it was very hard not to.

They turned onto Murkish Street and trudged down the block. "All right," said Trogg after a while. "We'll start here." They stopped beside a stationery store that Doon remembered had been closed long before people left Ember; its shelves held nothing but dust. "Upstairs," said Trogg, parking the wagon and leading the way to the apartment above. "Open everything," he instructed Doon. "Drawers, cabinets, cupboards, closets, everything. Pull all the stuff out, and we'll sort through it. Any eyeglasses you find, give them to me. I collect them."

"Why?" asked Doon.

"Because I want perfect vision, of course," said Trogg. "Not that there's anything *wrong* with my vision. But with the right pair of glasses, you can see for miles. Sometimes you can see in the dark. I just haven't found the right ones yet. Now get busy."

Doon followed instructions. Out came the possessions of whoever had lived here—sweaters, coats, mittens, scarves, underwear, teacups, soup spoons, knitting needles, salt shakers, bed pillows, bars of soap—and the three Troggs pawed through it. Kanza tried on clothes and looked at herself in the mirror. "Would this look good on me?" she said. "Or maybe this?"

"No more clothes!" bellowed Trogg. "You've got enough."

Yorick had a comment about everything he picked up. "This is a good knife—I'll keep it." He stuffed it into his bag. "These cups are useless. We already have some just like them." He tossed them away, one after another. Some rolled into a corner. Some shattered on the floor. "Look at this ugly shirt—who would have worn this?" He wadded it up and pitched it across the room.

In the kitchen, Trogg snatched up anything that looked edible and crammed it into his bag, sweeping the rest off the shelves. Empty cans and bottles and boxes fell to the floor, bouncing and breaking. Doon noticed that this family had still had a fair amount of food when they left the city—enough to keep a family in Sparks going for several days at least. He made a mental note. There might be many houses the Troggs had not yet looted.

"All right!" cried Trogg finally. "We're finished here. Load the stuff in the wagon, and on to the next."

It was like this the rest of the day. Doon followed along as they looted the homes and businesses of his former friends and neighbors. As they left each place, kicking aside the mess of scattered and broken belongings, Doon said a silent apology to the people who had lived there. They would never know their homes had been robbed and wrecked, nor would they know he had watched it being done. But even so, he felt sorry and guilty. He hated being part of this.

At the end of the day, the Troggs gathered around the fire in Harken Square. They all seemed excited. Doon saw that they were building the fire up higher than usual and that they'd set up a sort of rack at the edge of it—two piles of stones with a metal rod stretched between them, a curtain rod, maybe, or a pipe.

Yorick slouched up to his father. "Shall we go get it, Pa?" he said.

"Sure," said Trogg. "You go, too, Kanza, and help him. I'll stay here."

Yorick and Kanza went to the wagon loaded with the day's loot and tossed it all out onto the ground. Then they went off down Gilly Street, pulling the wagon behind them.

Doon became aware of Minny, standing a little distance away, saying something in a trembly voice. Trogg noticed her, too. "What, Min?" he said. "Speak up!"

She took a step forward and murmured some more, holding out a folded black cloth.

"Oh, the lightcap," said Trogg. "Well done!" He strode over and took it from her and handed it to Doon. "This is for you," he said. "Get one of those candles over there and stick it in this part." He pointed to the tube at the front.

Doon fetched a candle from a box of them behind the armchair. He held it to the fire to light it, and he put it in the cap and then put the cap on his head. It fit well and gave a useful amount of light. He wondered why no one in Sparks had yet thought up such a thing.

"Kanz and Yorick will be gone awhile," Trogg said. "In the meantime, you can help us get ready." He picked up a bucket and handed it to Doon. "We're going to need some more water. See that brown door over there? The one on the corner?" He pointed at an apartment on Gilly Street. "That's ours. Go upstairs and fill the bucket."

Doon was puzzled. "Upstairs? But—"

"Aha," said Trogg. "I know what you're thinking. When I first came to this place, I couldn't figure out where the water came from, either. I knew they must have had it. They had sinks; they had bathtubs. But where did the water come from?"

From the river, thought Doon.

"It was a good thing we'd brought some bottles of water with us," Trogg said, "because it took us a couple days of exploring to find it. But we did. You wouldn't believe what we found."

Doon waited.

"An underground river!" Trogg said. "Yes, it's true. We had to go down about a hundred steps to get to it. Did quite a bit of unpleasant cleanup on the way."

"Cleanup?" said Doon.

"Bodies," said Trogg. "Must have been some sort of stampede there, maybe as people were leaving the city. Quite a few dead folks lying around. We dragged them down the steps and shoved them in the river, and it swept them away." Trogg shook his head, wrinkling his nose in disgust.

Bodies, Doon thought. Trogg seemed to think of them as garbage. But they were citizens of Ember, people he'd probably known, caught in the panic of the last-minute exit. Inwardly, he winced in pain, thinking of it—but Trogg was going on. "So the river," he said. "When this city was in working order, the water was pumped up into the pipes that led to the houses. Now, of course, the pump doesn't work. No e-lec-tricity." He divided up the syllables, in case Doon had trouble understanding the word. "Have you heard of e-lec-tricity? It's a kind of magic. Very advanced. It's what makes the stars shine."

"I know about it," said Doon. He bit his tongue to keep from saying more.

"So," Trogg went on, "there was no way we could go down those steps every day and fetch up buckets of river water. I thought we were going to have to give up the whole project and leave. Then I remembered about the breathing." He looked up smugly at one of the streetlamps, as if he himself were responsible for its occasional glow. "When the electricity comes on," he said, "the pump comes on, too, right? Sometimes for just a few seconds, sometimes for minutes at a time. So in our apartment and a couple of the other ones on our street, we opened the taps and put the plugs in the sinks and the tubs, and whenever the city breathes, the water comes out. Not exactly a gusher, but a good enough trickle. In a few days, we have water to scoop up whenever we need it. What do you think of that, hah?"

"Clever," said Doon. It *was* clever. Trogg had a knack for figuring things out, Doon had to admit it. And yet he did not see Trogg as a truly intelligent person. Trogg seemed to think that he knew everything, but strangely enough, it was exactly this that made him seem stupid to Doon. A person who thought he knew everything simply didn't understand how much there was to know.

Doon took the bucket and trudged away toward the apartment Trogg had pointed out. Behind him, he heard Trogg's voice again. "Hey, you useless flump! Get a bucket and show that Dood where to go!"

Doon looked back. The thin boy had picked up a bucket and was lurching after him. Doon waited for him to catch up and followed him through the door, up the stairs, and into the apartment that had been turned into the dwelling place of the Trogg family.

He knew this place—it had been the home of one of his classmates, Orly Gordon, and Doon had been in it a few times during his school years. The rooms had been tidy then, although shabby, like everything in Ember. Now they were almost unrecognizable.

The Troggs must have searched dozens of apartments and dragged everything they liked best into this one. In the orange candlelight, he saw that the main room was crammed with furniture—there were five beds, six fat armchairs, a brown and orange striped couch piled with cushions and quilts and blankets, and three tables piled with dishes. Coats and sweaters and scarves and other clothes hung from hooks and were draped over the furniture. Countless boxes full of canned food stood in teetering stacks—the loot from a great many apartments.

The boy was making his way through this maze of stuff toward the bathroom. Doon followed him in and saw that murky water stood in the sink and filled about half of the bathtub. They bent over the tub and scooped their buckets in. Doon took a chance. He knew that the boy might tell on him to Trogg—but somehow he didn't think so. "Are they keeping you a prisoner here?" he asked.

The boy shook his head.

"But you don't *want* to be here, do you?"

"Yes, I do," said the boy, hoisting his bucket out of the water. He seemed barely strong enough to do it— his arms trembled.

Doon reached over and helped him lift. "But they treat you like a slave!" he said. "Wouldn't you leave if you could?"

Again, the boy just shook his head.

"If I could figure out how to get away," Doon said, "would you come with me?"

"I can't," the boy said, pointing down at his twisted leg. "I can't walk right."

"How did you get down here, then?" Doon asked.

"He took me on his back," said the boy.

"Trogg? So he does care about you, then?"

"A little," said the boy. "He's trying to make me strong."

"But he's so mean to you."

The boy nodded. "He took my treasures."

"Treasures?"

"Just some things I like. Things I've been collecting."

His eyes were so sad as he said this that Doon had to look away. He lifted his bucket, now full and heavy, out of the water. "Why did he take them?"

"I was defiant," said the boy.

Doon couldn't picture this timid little person being defiant. "You mean you talked back to him?"

"No, no. I just didn't jump up fast enough when he told me to."

"What's your name?" Doon asked.

The boy kept his eyes on the murky water. "He

gave me a new name," he said. He heaved up his full bucket and headed for the door.

Doon clanked after him. "You could help me find the key," he said. "If I could get this chain off, I could get away and bring someone to rescue you."

The boy didn't answer. Water from his bucket sloshed out as he struggled toward the stairs. At the top step, he turned his head halfway toward Doon. "He put my treasures on the top shelf," he said. "I can't reach them."

"The top shelf of what?"

"In the kitchen." The boy set his bucket down, lowered his bad leg onto the first step, got his other leg down with a little hop, picked up the bucket and moved it down one step, and repeated the ungainly process all the way down the stairs.

Doon followed. They lugged their buckets of water in silence, and when they got to the bonfire, they emptied them, according to Trogg's instructions, into a big pot, which Trogg set on the fire.

Then they waited. The lame boy sat on the ground, leaning against a pile of sacks with his knees up and his chin on his knees. He stared into the fire without moving. Minny puttered around making dinner preparations, and Trogg sat in an armchair, sipping from a cup of water he'd scooped from the washtub, and made Doon sit on the ground beside him. "The day will come," Trogg said, "when you'll realize how lucky you were to join up with us here in Darkhold. When that happens, we can get rid of this." He reached down and jangled the chain that bound Doon's feet. Minny, who was going by at the time with a sack of potatoes, jumped at the sound. "Of course, we have to be very, very sure," said Trogg, "before that can happen."

That would be one way out, thought Doon—to pretend that he was happy to be here and wouldn't want to run away. But it would take a long time to prove that to Trogg. Doon thought of Lina, alone now, and of his father, injured and disabled. He thought of the people in Sparks, who had so little to get by on for the winter. He thought of the ancient book about something meant for the people of Ember, something he was longing to find. And most of all, he thought of the great sunlit world—he would rather be there and hungry than here and fed. There wasn't time to pretend he'd grown happy with the Troggs. He had to get away now.

CHAPTER 11

The Shepherd

As soon as she'd waved at Doon and the lights had gone out again, Lina started on her return journey. The first task was to find her way out through the Unknown Regions to the place where the path led up along the cave wall. Using her third match, she lit a candle and went back through Ember the way she'd come, repeating to herself, in reverse order, the names of the streets she'd traveled, and in a few minutes she found herself once again on the corner where the white rocking chair stood. That chair, she thought, must be here on purpose. It must be here to mark the place where you go out.

So she ventured forward, stepping from the paved street onto the bare pebble-strewn ground. She moved slowly, keeping her eyes on the circle of candlelight beneath her feet. There was no way to know if she was walking toward the bottom of the path; she would just have to hope that if she went directly away from the city, she would come to it. She put one foot ahead of the other, feeling as if she had to push back a wall of darkness with every step.

An empty can appeared just in front of her right foot, and she kicked it without meaning to. Startled, she stopped. When she moved her candle a bit to the right, she saw another empty can lying on its side. She remembered: on the way in, they'd seen cans and broken jars. She'd thought they were litter, but what if they were markers? What if those people who had taken over the city had put them here so they could find their way to the path?

It made sense. She began to look for them. Soon she saw that each bit of junk was just a few steps beyond the last. Every time she came to one, if she took four or five steps beyond it, she would see the next. In this way, she arrived after a while at the spot she dreaded most: the plank bridge that crossed the chasm.

She stood for quite a while just looking at it: the two splintery boards reaching out into the dark and the ghastly drop below. I can't do it, she thought. I have to turn around and go back, and try to rescue Doon some other way.

But there *was* no other way; she knew that. She would have to reach into herself and find the courage to cross that bridge. It must be there somewhere.

She closed her eyes, felt her heart beating, felt her feet planted firmly on the rocky ground. She tried to find her best self, and she remembered: She was fast; she was sure-footed. These narrow boards would be nothing to her if they lay across a stream or even stretched from the roof of one building to the roof of another. It wasn't the bridge that scared her; it was what lay beneath. She would have to block the pit of bones from her mind and be her messenger self again, stopping at nothing to make an urgent delivery. She took a long breath, gripped her candle, fixed her eyes on the boards, and stepped onto them. Without pausing for even a second, she sped across the pit with a swift, steady stride. When she reached the other bank, she ran a few steps and then stopped, breathed again, and waited while her heart crashed around in her chest and her whole body trembled.

Then she went on her way, and before too long, she came to the place where the path began to slope upward along the cave wall.

It was a lonely, frightening walk, but almost easy compared to getting across the pit. Halfway up, when she was so high that she was once more looking down at the spot of fire glowing in the center of the city, her candle burned low and grew too warm to hold. She jammed it into a crack in the rocky wall beside her, and with shaky hands, she pulled another candle from her pack and held its wick to the flame. Here on this uneven ledge, with a steep drop inches away, she did not want to be left in total darkness even for a moment.

The climb seemed endless. Her legs began to ache, and the sound of her own hard breathing filled her ears. All the way, the image of Doon captured and tied up stayed with her, a terrible picture burned into her mind. She should have paid attention to her bad feeling about coming here. It was a mistake, a dreadful mistake.

But there was no point in thinking about that now. She was coming to the top of the path at last—she could tell by how far above the spot of light she was. And sure enough, a few more steps and she found herself on the ledge, with the entrance to the passage on her right. She sidled through and came out into the clean, cold air of the upper world.

The sun, low and red in the sky, blinded her for a moment. She could tell that it was late afternoon— maybe four o'clock or even later. Not much daylight was left. Could she find her way back to Sparks in the dark? She couldn't bear leaving Doon a prisoner a second longer than she had to. She imagined how desperate he must be feeling. He wouldn't even know if she'd got safely out of the cave. He might think she'd fallen into the pit or slipped off the edge of the path on the way up. She had to hurry.

So she retrieved the rolled-up blankets and supplies they'd left between the rocks and stuffed them into her pack. She began to walk, heading down around the mountain the way they'd come.

She'd gone no more than twenty steps when exhaustion washed over her like a wave. Her legs wobbled; her head felt heavy. There was no way around it: she would have to rest before she could go on. She staggered a little farther and made it to the main cave entrance. Inside, she threw a blanket on the ground, flopped down upon it, and went instantly to sleep.

When she awoke, the daylight was nearly gone, and somewhere not far away, someone was shouting. Lina scrambled to her feet, snatched up the blanket, and hurried out into the open. There she saw a startling sight: a tented wagon drawn by a scrawny horse. Beside it walked some sheep and a shepherd who Lina recognized right away: it was the roamer who had come to Sparks.

"Hey!" the shepherd shouted, starting toward Lina, coming through the flock of sheep, poking them out of the way with her long stick. The sheep bleated and sidestepped nervously.

Lina ran forward. "Please help me!" she cried. "I have to get home! I have to hurry!" In a rush, the awfulness of her situation came over her: Doon a prisoner, the sun going down, the long walk ahead. Her heart began to hammer.

The shepherd came closer. Her eyes were a watery

blue in the red of her face, and her nose showed a network of fine red lines. "Are you lost? Are you a runaway?" She tilted her head and peered hard at Lina. "Haven't I seen you before?"

"Yes," said Lina. "I saw you in Sparks, where I live. That's where I'm going. I have to get there tonight."

The shepherd poked her stick at the rear end of a sheep that had separated itself from the rest. "Get back here, you filthy fluffball!" she yelled. Then she pointed the stick at Lina. "You," she said, "are a foolish child. You can't possibly get there tonight. What are you doing up here, anyhow, so far from home?"

The words spilled out of Lina in a rush. "We came to our old city, looking for things, but there are people living there, and they captured Doon! I have to get help for him!"

"Your old city?" said the shepherd.

"Yes, underground!" Lina's voice was shaking. "Awful people have taken it over."

"Captured your friend, you say?"

"Yes, tied him up!"

The shepherd crooked a corner of her mouth and shook her head. "Up to his mischief," she muttered.

Before Lina could ask what she meant, the shepherd turned away abruptly. One of her sheep was wandering off. She strode after it and gave it a whack with her stick to steer it back toward the flock. "Move, fuzzface!" she yelled at it, and the sheep put its head down in a sorrowful way and trotted toward its companions.

Lina felt more and more desperate. How could she get this woman to help her? She saw that lanterns hung from the front and back of her wagon. There was even a lantern dangling from the side of the horse. So maybe the shepherd could travel at night. Besides, she'd been to Sparks before. She knew how to get there. "Could I go with you?" Lina called, running after the shepherd, who was still dealing with the wayward sheep. "Could you take me back to Sparks tonight?"

"I don't travel at night."

"But you could," Lina said. "You have lanterns. You know the way."

"I *could*," said the shepherd. "But I don't want to. Too hard and too dangerous. Wolves out there, you know. I heard them howling just a little while ago. Besides, it's going to rain." She tilted her head toward the clouds at the horizon. "Anyhow, I'm not going that direction. I'm heading due south tomorrow. Just made my last delivery." She thumped her stick on the ground. "He can get his own, after this," she said. "Maggs is quitting!"

"Quitting what?" Maggs, Lina assumed, must be the shepherd's name.

"Quitting this job of food-finder. I'm sick of it. It's cold and miserable up here, and nobody in the towns has anything to trade with, and I'm through."

Lina was confused. "Finding food for who?"

The shepherd flung up her arms, and her raggedy sleeves flapped in the wind. "My brother! King of the Underground!" she cried. "That's what he's made himself. And I'm supposed to drop down supplies for a few months and then go down there and join them. Well, I've decided I don't want to. Especially if he's taken to kidnapping people." She shouted at her flock again, which had drifted away. "Scurvy beasts! Wretched meatbrains! Get back here!" She flailed her stick at them. The horse lowered its head and ripped up a mouthful of grass.

"You mean," said Lina, putting all this together, "that's *your brother* down there? That awful man?"

"He's not *that* awful," Maggs said. "He's gotten too high and mighty, is the problem. Too set on having his perfect little world, all for himself."

Lina was paying attention now. "How do you deliver food to him?"

"Just drop it down," said Maggs, gesturing behind her in the direction of the crack in the mountainside. "You may not know this," she said, "but I am a kind and caring person. If I could, I would let my brother know he's just had his last

132

delivery, and he's on his own now. But if you think I'm going down into that dark old cave to tell him, you can think again."

"Why didn't you write him a message," Lina asked, "when you made the delivery?"

"Write?" said Maggs. "I don't write."

"You mean you don't know how?"

The shepherd shrugged and scowled. "Never wanted to," she said.

An idea began to form in Lina's mind. "I could help you," she said. "If you take me back toward Sparks tonight, even just part of the way, I would write a message for you to send to your brother."

"No point in that," Maggs said. "He can't read."

The wind turned colder and rustled the leaves of the trees. The red light in the west faded to a dusty orange, streaked with dark purple clouds. Lina thought fast. "I could *draw* the message," she said.

"I told you," said Maggs. "I don't travel at night."

"But it isn't *quite* night yet," Lina said. "We could go at least a little way."

"Not very far," said Maggs.

"Please," said Lina. "I'll draw a really good message for your brother. Watch. I'll do it."

Lina pulled her pencil stub and a scrap of paper from her pack. "I need something flat to draw on," she said. Maggs unhooked a bucket that hung from the side of her wagon and turned it upside down. Lina drew this:

DOON- OUT SAFELY,
HEADING HOME TO SPARKS — L.

"You put words on it," Maggs said. "I told you he can't read."

"Oh," said Lina. "I forgot. Well, it doesn't matter. The drawing is clear without them."

"What do they say?" the shepherd asked.

"They say, 'Brother—I'm quitting. Get your own food. —M.'"

Maggs put a finger on the last letter. "That isn't *M*," she said. "I know *M* when I see it."

"Oh, oops," Lina said. "I wrote it wrong." She added a big *M* right next to the *L*, thankful that her last name was Mayfleet. "Now," she said, "all you have to do is wrap it in a rag, and put a rock with it, and throw it down where you dropped your supplies." Maggs reached for the message, but Lina pulled it back. "You have to promise to take me home," she said.

"Sorry," said Maggs. "The answer is no. I'm not going your direction anyway. I'm heading south. You need to go southwest."

"Oh, *please,*" Lina said. "It's so important!"

"Can't do it," said Maggs. "I'll tell you what, though."

"What?"

"You can walk with me until it's dark and then camp with me tonight. Sleep in the wagon, out of the rain."

"But that will take me the wrong direction, out of my way."

"Not far," said Maggs. "It won't be more than half an hour before it's dark and we have to stop."

It was so terribly frustrating—Lina wanted to *go,* to *travel,* right now. But it was just not possible, unless she wanted to risk never getting home at all. She would have to accept Maggs's offer, even though it would take her out of her way and she'd need to backtrack some in the morning. "All right," she said. She held out her drawing, but just as Maggs's hand reached for it, she snatched it back again. Another idea had struck her. Only her panic had kept her from thinking of it before. "That book!" she said. "That book you sold to my friend Doon! I'll give you my drawing if you'll tell me where you found it."

Maggs shrugged. "Sure," she said. "No reason not to, if you already know about that underground city. Give me the message, and then I'll show you the place."

Lina handed it over.

The shepherd went to the back of her wagon and burrowed around inside. Lina could hear her humming, and now and then the hum became a song with a few mumbly words. It was the same tune Maggs had been humming the first day she came to Sparks, the tune Lina had recognized from somewhere. What was it?

When Maggs emerged, carrying a greasy rag, Lina asked her.

"Oh, an old song that lots of roamers know," Maggs said. "It used to be a sort of riddle, but it isn't anymore. Not to me."

"Will you sing it for me?" Lina asked.

In her croaky voice, Maggs sang:

"There's buried treasure in the ancient city.
Remember, remember, from times of old.
What's hidden will come to light again,
A diamond jewel more precious than gold."

Maggs grinned. "The reason it's not a mystery is, we found the city, me and my family, and we found the diamond, too. Hah! So the riddle's solved." She tied up Lina's message in her rag, along with a rock. "I'll go toss it down," she said. She handed Lina her stick. "You keep an eye on these woolies; don't let them stray."

Lina watched as she trudged up the mountainside

toward the crack in the wall. She pondered the song. It was the one she'd heard from the roamer on the way back from her journey to the ruined city during the summer. The same song—and yet something was different about the way Maggs sang it. The words weren't exactly the same, were they? Lina couldn't remember. But she was too cold and tired to think about it now. She crossed her arms over her chest, hugging herself against the wind, which was gaining force. If I'm lucky, she thought, Doon will see that message and know that help is coming. And I'll know where Maggs found the book that got us into all this trouble.

CHAPTER 12

Feast Night

Doon sat glumly on an old armchair that smelled of ashes and watched as Minny worked on the fire. She scraped at it with a rake that must have come from one of the greenhouses, pulling coals toward the rod they'd set up over two stacks of stones. Every time she came near Doon, she skittered past without looking at him, as if she was afraid he might stick his legs out and trip her. She fluttered her hands, patted her chest, and plucked at the hair at the back of her neck. She was the most nervous, twittery person Doon had ever seen. Trogg directed her with waves of his arms and shouts. "More fuel over there! Bank it up here! Quicker, Minny! Stop flittering!"

Behind Minny, the lame boy drifted silently around, fetching and carrying when she told him to.

"What's his name?" Doon asked Trogg, pointing to the boy.

"Scawgo," said Trogg. "He had another name, but I changed it to go with the names of my kids." He turned away from the fire and planted himself in front of Doon. "See, I've picked up a lot of information about the ancient world in my time. Want to know anything, just ask me. I named my kids after ancient cities. There was New Yorick, and there was Kanza City, and there was Scawgo. Of course, lots of others. But I like the sound of those. Gave my wife a new name, too. She used to be Cora; now she's Minny, after a city called Minny-Apple. In those ancient places, Drood," he said, "there was *power*. I honor power. I draw it toward me, as I am a naturally powerful person." He stood tall and puffed his chest out. "I chose my own name," he said, "from the most powerful city of all: Washton. "

Doon remembered looking at the map in the book Edward Pocket had shown him. He was pretty sure that Trogg didn't have the names of the cities quite right. "In a book I read—" he said, but Trogg interrupted him.

"Oh, books," said Trogg. "Used to be very useful."

"Yes," said Doon. "So if you looked in this book, you could see that those cities' names were actually—"

"I mean useful for fuel," Trogg said. "Pretty much gone now, though. We burned 'em up ages ago, where I come from."

"Burned them up?" Doon was horrified. "Why?"

"Because what's the point of them? Full of squiggles. People have a lot more important things to deal with than figuring out squiggles. Matters of survival, Droon."

"But in books, you can find out what people have discovered. You can find out how things work, and—"

Trogg pointed a finger at Doon. "You listen to me," he said. "We know how things work. We don't need any squiggles to tell us."

"But if you would just even read the names of the cities—" Doon began.

"We don't read," said Trogg shortly. "So quit yapping about it. We don't approve of reading; we stopped doing it long ago. It's a useless trick. Everything we need to know came down to us from our fathers and our grandfathers and their fathers before them."

Doon understood. Where Trogg came from, people didn't know *how* to read. He blinked in amazement, but he didn't say any more about it.

Minny bent over the pot of water, poking a long fork at the potatoes boiling in there. She seemed to be afraid of Doon. When he clanked over to look at what was cooking, she edged away from him, her hand fluttering at her throat, her face turned away. Doon went back to the smelly armchair and sat down to wait.

Trogg bent over a box of stuff near the fire and burrowed through it, tossing things out left and right, muttering furiously. "It's not here," he said at last, resting back on his heels. "Minny! Where's that little bottle of salt?"

Minny and Scawgo were sitting facing each other, with a short board between them on which they were chopping up some soggy-looking onions. She glanced up at Trogg with tears dripping from her eyes and said, "It's upstairs, husband. In the kitchen."

"We need it," Trogg said, glaring at her and Scawgo.

"Of course," said Minny. "We'll just put this down—don't let that onion roll off, Scawgo. Hold the board steady—whoops, the knife is sliding—"

"Never mind!" Trogg bellowed. "I'll send the new boy." He turned to Doon and stared hard at him. "Go upstairs," he said. "Get the little green bottle from the table in the kitchen. Do not even *think* about touching anything else. You will be searched when you return."

So Doon hobbled off toward the apartment and climbed the stairs, his chain clanking the whole way. He found the bottle of salt on the table and put it into his pocket. Now. He was alone; no one was watching him. There must be some way he could use this moment. Could he go out a back window? But with his feet chained, he wouldn't be able to land right. The two-story drop would probably break his ankles or wrists. Could he steal something useful, some kind of weapon, a knife, a hammer? But Trogg was going to search him; he'd find it right away. What else, what else? Doon swept his eyes around the apartment—the main room with its beds and couches and armchairs all crowded together at crazy angles, the kitchen with dirty mugs standing on the table, and smeared spoons, and the cabinets full of bottles and cans . . .

A thought came to him. The kitchen was where Trogg had stashed Scawgo's treasures. Up high somewhere. If Doon couldn't help himself here, maybe he could help the boy. Quickly, he flung open the doors of all the upper cabinets to see what was on their top shelves. Nothing in the first one, nothing in the second, but in the third, he saw a cloth sack way up on an otherwise empty shelf near the ceiling. He'd have to guess that it held Scawgo's little collection.

He dragged a chair over to the kitchen counter. If his feet hadn't been chained, he could easily have stepped onto the chair and from there to the counter. But the chain made it impossible to separate his feet enough to get one of them onto the chair at a time. So, with both hands on the counter, he hoisted himself up, bending his knees until his feet rested on the chair's seat. When he stood up and raised an arm, he found the top shelf still out of reach. He turned around with small clanking steps, sat on the counter, swung his feet up, and with some difficulty stood up again. This time, stretching his arm high, he managed to grab the sack with two fingers. He pulled on it and caught it as it fell.

Once he was down again, he took just enough time for one glimpse inside the sack—he saw something glittery and some papers—to feel sure enough that he'd got the right thing. Then he crossed the room with it and pushed the sack deep under the striped couch.

Back down the stairs—the quickest way was to sit down and slide—and out to the fire, where he handed Trogg the salt bottle.

"Took you a while," Trogg said.

"Chained feet," said Doon. "*You* should try it."

Trogg patted him all over to make sure he hadn't stolen anything, and Doon sat down again in the smelly chair and continued to wait for dinner.

Finally, on Gilly Street, he saw the two lights that meant Yorick and Kanza were coming back. It was clear from their excited cries that whatever they'd brought with them was dinner.

"We got it, Pa!" Yorick exclaimed as they pulled the wagon up close. "It was just where it was supposed to be. A bunch of other stuff, too."

Minny peered into the wagon and nodded. "Mmm-hmm," she said. "Yes, very good, oh, very good."

"So let's get going!" cried Kanza. "I'm starving!"

Doon got up out of the chair to take a closer look. In the wagon, he saw some lumpy sacks and also what seemed at first to be a heap of wool.

Yorick reached in and with a grunt lifted the wool in his arms. Doon saw a head, and legs hanging down. A sheep! he thought. No, a lamb—it was smaller than a full-grown sheep. And it didn't move; it was asleep or dead. Where had it come from? Had they gone up out of the cave to get it?

Yorick and his father laid the lamb down on the pavement not far from where Doon was sitting. Minny and Kanza stood nearby. From a bucket full of tools, Trogg took a couple of long knives, and he and his son set to work cutting off the lamb's head. They cut off the four hooves next, kicking them aside, and then, with great wrenchings and gruntings, they peeled away the woolly skin until the lamb was a slippery red slab with sticklike stumps where the head and legs used to be.

Doon knew that people ate animals. They never had in Ember; there *were* no animals there. But in Sparks, in the winter, his father had now and then brought home from the market some chunks of chewy, salty stuff that was called meat. Doon had been astonished when he was told it was made from animals and had been saddened as well; the animals were new and fascinating creatures to him, and it was hard to accept that they were killed for food.

Now, watching the Troggs turn the lamb into meat, he had to press his hands against his mouth to keep from making a sound.

While Trogg was cutting up the lamb, Yorick and Kanza heaved the sacks out of the wagon and opened them. Inside were a lot of potatoes with dirt still on them; a few big, flabby cabbages; and several smaller sacks that Yorick peered into, announcing the contents of each: "Dried corn. Some kind of beans. Some kind of grain. Ewww! Mushrooms."

Kanza held up a small rag bundle. "This was on top of the rest," she said. "It's tied in a knot."

"Well, *untie* it, picklenose," said Trogg, who was busy sticking the lamb's body onto the skewer over the fire.

Kanza opened the bundle. "A rock," she said. "We have enough rocks, if you ask me."

But something fluttered out—a scrap of paper. Kanza stooped to pick it up. She squinted at it. "It's a picture," she said. "Look, Pa."

Trogg came over to see. So did Minny, hugging herself with her skinny arms as she passed Doon. Yorick peered over Kanza's shoulder, and Doon, too, clanked over to see.

"There's words on it," said Yorick.

"Someone else must have written them for her," Trogg said. "Strange. Why would she want *words*? Who would be up there anyway?"

"So what does it mean, Pa?" asked Kanza.

Trogg took the candle from his cap and held it near the paper. "It means," he said. Then he was silent for a while. "It means she is going away."

"Oh, alas!" cried Minny. "Leaving us? For good?"

"Well, who knows?" Trogg said. "Looks like it, though. She's waving."

"But what about the words, Pa?" asked Kanza.

"Pass it over to him," Trogg said, nodding toward Doon. "He likes to waste his time with words."

Kanza handed Doon the paper. Silently, he read the message.

"So?" said Kanza. "What does it say?"

With an effort, Doon kept himself from smiling. He could see that Trogg was listening, though he was pretending not to, so he had to think of something fast. He frowned over the words, as if he was having trouble making them out. The curly bits of the drawing were clearly sheep. The person who was dropping supplies from up above must be a shepherd. It did look as if the shepherd was waving goodbye. He thought of making up something that might help him, such as, RELEASE THAT BOY IMMEDIATELY! Or GET OUT! BANDITS COMING! But he had to make the words go with the picture, or they wouldn't believe him. Best to play it safe, he finally decided. "It says, 'Goodbye! I'm leaving. No more from me.'"

Minny wailed.

"Don't be an idiot," Trogg said. "Who cares? We've got enough for a long time. Don't forget what we found the other day."

"Oh, yes," said Minny, cheering up.

"What did you find?" asked Doon.

"A little hole-in-the-wall shop over that way," said Trogg, waving a hand.

"No sign on it or anything," put in Kanza.

"Nothing in front at all. Shelves empty. But the back room was absolutely crammed with good stuff," Trogg said. "*Someone* was hoarding."

"Oh," said Doon, filing this information away in his mind. "Excellent."

All this time, the lamb roasted over the fire, and a smell that Doon found part sickening and part delicious wafted toward him. At last Trogg and Minny took the brown and glistening hulk down from its stick, and Trogg set upon it again with a knife, carving it into chunks, which were snatched up with great gusto by his family and bitten and gnawed until nothing was left but bones. They threw the bones in the fire and wiped their greasy faces on their sleeves.

Doon ate the meat, too. He was very hungry, but still he took the hot chunk from Trogg with two fingers only, like something dangerous or repulsive. It had a rubbery texture and a greasy taste. He ate every bite.

CHAPTER 13

The Diamond

The Trogg family sat around the fire for quite a while after dinner. Their full bellies made them jolly in a rough sort of way, and they burped and chortled and told jokes that made no sense to Doon. Trogg launched into a lecture about the nature of the universe, on which subject he considered himself an expert. He said it was a perfect sphere, like a bubble, with the earth exactly in the center. The sky was exactly a hundred miles up, he said, and the stars were lit by electricity. "You probably don't know this," he remarked with a nod at Doon, "but sometimes a new star shows up. I have seen such a one recently myself—a greenish star that moves."

"We all saw it," said Yorick. "Just before we came in here."

Minny murmured, "Yes, we saw it, we did." Her

eyes were half closed; she looked ready to fall asleep in her chair.

Trogg went on for a while about how the moon was actually much larger than it looked, about the size of a wagon wheel, and how the earth, if you could view it from far above, would look like a vast dinner plate, exactly a million times bigger than the moon. "And the mountains would look like lumps of mashed potatoes!" said Yorick. "And the forests would look like spinach!" said Kanza, and they both broke down into great guffaws.

Finally, Trogg pointed to the hourglass, which was draining its last grains of sand into its bottom half. "Bedtime!" he cried. Minny awoke with a start, and everyone got up and shuffled off to the apartment.

There Minny hurried around sticking candles in cups and cans. Their orange glow cast flickering shadows of the great piles of stuff that cluttered the room.

"That's where you sleep," said Trogg to Doon, pointing to a brown and orange striped couch, which had a couple of blankets draped over it. Scawgo went from one bed to the next, folding and smoothing blankets.

"Scawgo hardly ever speaks," Doon observed.

"He speaks when spoken to," said Trogg. "A good rule for everyone."

"I don't agree," said Doon.

"What's that?" Trogg stopped in his tracks and

put one big hand behind his big ear, as if having hearing difficulties.

"I said, I don't agree that it's good to speak only when spoken to." Suddenly Doon could feel his temper rising in him like a spurt of flame, even though he knew that contradicting Trogg was probably dangerous. "If everyone did that, no one would ever speak at all! What you mean is that people should only speak when *you* speak to them. Because you're so powerful, I guess. Why do *you* get to be the powerful one?"

Trogg's face bunched up in fury, and he took a threatening step toward Doon. Everyone else suddenly stopped talking and looked up. Trogg paused. His expression changed. His mouth stretched into a smile. "Dood," he said, "that is a good question. What makes me powerful? I will tell you. A powerful person is one who takes action. I have taken drastic action to make sure my family is safe from danger. A powerful person is one who is strong. You know that I am strong. Extraordinary things fall into the path of a powerful person, and into my path came this city—and something else as well." Without taking his eyes off Doon, Trogg beckoned to Yorick. "Get the jewel, Yor," he said. "We'll show this impudent mophead what we mean by power."

"Are you sure, Pa?" said Yorick. "What if he—"

"Of course I'm sure, bone-brain! Get it out!"

Yorick went to the door of a closet, opened it, and reached inside. He brought out a bundle, wrapped in a yellow rag. It was about the size of a large potato. Yorick handed it to his father. The other members of the family clustered around, including Scawgo. Whatever this was, Doon could see they were proud of it. Minny pressed her hands together beneath her chin, and her lips trembled as if she were whispering to herself. Kanza smirked and slewed her eyes toward Doon, clearly expecting him to be awestruck.

"This," said Trogg, "was waiting to be found for an eon of time. It was waiting for the right person, and that person turned out to be myself, W. Trogg. This is how fate arranges things: to the powerful person comes the extraordinary discovery." He began to unwind the cloth from whatever was inside it. "Do you know the meaning of the word 'jewel,' boy?"

Doon nodded. His heart gave a jump. Could this be one of the jewels mentioned in the book of eight pages?

"Well," said Trogg, "this is a jewel unlike any ever seen before." He let the cloth fall away, and he held the jewel in his two hands. "Minny!" he called. "Bring a couple of candles here so this boy can see."

The jewel was a deep, clear blue. At first sight, Doon thought it was a smooth oval, about six inches high. But when he looked closer, he could see that its many sides were flat, with angles between them. The candlelight sparkled on every edge. At the jewel's base was a golden ring, like a neck. Doon bent to look closely and saw that within the glassy depths were thousands of tiny bits, like splintered blue ice, each one separately catching the light and making the whole jewel shimmer and gleam, a stone full of stars. It was a beautiful thing, and he could believe that it was powerful in some way. It seemed to enclose a mystery. In Trogg's big grubby hands, it looked all wrong. Doon had an urge to take it from him—not to steal it, but to rescue it. He reached out to touch it.

Trogg snatched it away. "No touching!" he cried. "Just look. Hands off."

"What is it?" Doon asked.

"I told you, Droon," said Trogg. "It's a kind of jewel. It's called a diamond."

"But what is it good for?"

Trogg gave an exasperated sigh. "It is a *marvel*," he said. "People will give a lot just to lay eyes on it. Someday, if we want to, we can trade this for just about anything."

"A stone house on a mountaintop," said Yorick.

"With land all around and a high wall," added his mother. "Oh, such a high wall." She sighed and twisted her fingers together.

"And servants to do the work, and animals, and all the clothes we want," said Kanza.

Doon wasn't listening. He was sure of it now. This was it. This diamond was what the book was about. A tingling wave swept through him, and for a moment he forgot to breathe. "Are there more of them?" he asked.

"Of course not!" thundered Trogg. "Want one for yourself, don't you? Well, you're too late. This is the one and only."

"Where did you get it?" Doon asked.

"Just up there," said Trogg, flicking his thumb upward toward the blackness overhead. "Right by the—"

"Don't tell, don't tell!" cried Yorick.

His father gave him a scornful look. "And why not?"

"Because . . . because it's a secret," Yorick said lamely.

"It *was* a secret," Trogg corrected. "A secret waiting for us. It's nothing now, just an empty room."

"Outside, you mean?" Doon asked. He'd expected to hear that Trogg had found it in the storerooms. "Up on top?"

Trogg nodded. "Built into the mountainside," he said. "By the ancients. Probably this jewel was like a god to them, and they came there to worship it." He picked up the cloth and rewrapped the diamond. "Do you know what a god is?" he said to Doon.

Doon said he did not.

"A god is the most powerful person there is. A god can rule an entire city, or an entire world. A god has riches, including jewels. So." He grinned. His chin jutted out, and his chest swelled. "Who does that remind you of?"

Doon didn't answer. But Trogg didn't seem to need an answer—he was quite sure of the answer himself. He handed the bundled-up diamond to Yorick. "Put it away," he said. "And you, Doob, don't think you will be left in here alone for even one fraction of a second. You won't have the slightest chance to get your hands on our diamond."

"I'm not a thief," said Doon.

Trogg raised his voice. "All right! Everyone to bed. Minny, you're on fire watch, first shift. Get down there."

Minny put on a coat and hurried downstairs.

"What's fire watch?" asked Doon.

"Watching the fire, of course," Trogg snapped. "So it doesn't go out. It might be your turn someday, when we know we can trust you."

Kanza went into one of the bedrooms. Yorick stretched out on a bed at the back of the room, and Scawgo lay down on a bed not far from the couch and drew his knees up near his chin. Doon took off his jacket. Reluctantly, he settled on the couch and pulled up the blanket, which stank of mildew.

"Everyone tucked in?" called Trogg.

"Yes, Pa," said Kanza's voice from the bedroom.

"Uh-huh," said Yorick, back by the kitchen.

Scawgo and Doon said nothing.

"Just a word of warning to you, young Doom," Trogg said. "No point trying to creep out of here in the night. We'll hear that chain going clinkety-clank." He took his candle into the other bedroom. There was some rustling and creaking and muttering, and then the light went out, and the room sank into a darkness as black as the dread and despair Doon felt inside.

"Sweet dreams," called Trogg.

Doon lay there wide awake. His mind went over and over the same thoughts, until he was afraid they were going to burn a hole in his head: How could he have been so stupid as to let himself be caught? Why hadn't it occurred to him that there might be danger down here? If he'd been paying better attention, would this have happened? Where was Lina on this night? Was she all right? If she wasn't, it was his fault.

In between these tormenting thoughts, he kept picturing the blue diamond, which was meant, he was *sure*, for the people of Ember. It was beautiful and mysterious. It had a purpose; he was sure it did, and he was sure that Trogg didn't know what that purpose was. But *I* could know, Doon thought. If I could only get my hands on it and really look at it, I could know.

He turned over, kicking at the blankets that twisted around his feet. The chain clinked.

Trogg's voice came in the dark. "Settle down."

"I might be able to sleep if you'd take this chain off me," Doon said.

"No chance," Trogg said. "Don't want you walking in your sleep, ha-ha."

A long time went by. Trogg snored—a snort, a growl, and a wheeze. Yorick breathed steadily, whistling now and then through his nose. Kanza muttered in her sleep from the next room. Scawgo, on his bed a few feet away, seemed to be still awake, making whimpery noises. Doon thought maybe he was talking to himself, since he didn't get to talk much to anyone else; or maybe he was crying.

He tried again to talk to him. "Scawgo," he whispered.

The whimpering stopped.

"Scawgo," said Doon again. "Scawgo, answer me."

From the direction of Scawgo came a tiny frantic sound: "Shh! Shh! Shh!"

Doon made his whisper even quieter. "Do you know what that diamond is?" No answer. "Listen to me," Doon said. "You don't have to say anything. Look under this couch, sometime when you're alone. I've put something there."

The couch sagged in the middle. Doon twisted this way and that, tangling himself in the thin blanket, trying to find a comfortable position. He had to get out of here. And that meant he had to find the key to the chain that bound his feet.

CHAPTER 14

Something Strange

Kenny Parton wasn't feeling very good. He was a little bit cold and a little bit hungry nearly all the time, and this was disagreeable, but even worse was the general dullness of everything. School, where he went a few days a week, seemed like a waste of good time. Most days, there were hardly any students. They stayed home to help care for sick brothers and sisters and grandparents, or to help repair leaking roofs, or because they weren't feeling well themselves. The students who did come often dozed off during the lessons. Still, the teacher, Eenette Buloware, showed up almost every day. For three hours in the morning, she told them stories from history or explained how things in the world worked. She had flimsy gray hair and a long neck and nervous hands that moved around in the air as if trying to draw pictures of what she was talking about.

"Today," she would say, "we are going to discuss Ancient Forms of Transportation," and her right hand, with its forefinger pointing, would travel out to her right side, weave back to the left, and move right again, in case anyone didn't know that transportation had to do with moving around. She would make a hand fly over her head when she talked about airplanes, and she would chug her elbows back and forth when she talked about trains.

Their lesson that day was on Appliances of the Ancient World. They would learn about this, Ms. Buloware said, because someday they would learn how to make these helpful things again. "Some of you in this very classroom," she said, "might learn to make a washing machine, or a stove, or a flush toilet."

"What is a flush toilet?" asked one of the smallest students.

Some of the others snickered, but Ms. Buloware was not embarrassed by this subject. "A flush toilet," she said, "causes human waste to be swept cleanly away. You can see them in the rooms at the Pioneer Hotel. They are white, shaped like a very large bowl, with a sort of box at the back." She made the shape of a bowl with her hands, and then the shape of a box.

"But how does it work?" said someone.

"Water springs up in it," said Ms. Buloware. "The water carries away the waste." Her hand swept sideways.

"And then where does it go?"

Ms. Buloware looked momentarily confused. Kenny could tell that she didn't know the answer to this question. She could have admitted this and no one would have blamed her. But she didn't like to appear ignorant. So she said, "It goes far, far away."

"But how?" Kenny asked.

Ms. Buloware frowned. "It has to do with pipes," she said. "And pressures. And electricity. In any case, it is too complex for me to explain to you."

It seemed to Kenny that everything in the Ancient World had to do with electricity. Whenever he asked how something had worked—cars, lamps, refrigerators, telescopes—the answer was always electricity. But then when he asked what electricity was, and where it came from, and why they couldn't get it now, Ms. Buloware never knew the answer. None of his other teachers had ever known it, either. Kenny figured that everything that seemed impossible had to do with electricity. He asked the teacher once if birds could fly because of electricity. "Of course not," she said. "Birds can fly because they have wings. And because they're alive. It isn't electricity that powers them."

"What does, then?" Kenny had asked, but the teacher just shook her head impatiently.

Another teacher, who'd read one of the books from the library Edward Pocket was making at the back of the Ark, said electricity came from lightning. But how you could take a great dagger of lightning that lasted for only a few seconds and use it to make a lamp light up Kenny could not understand. He liked things to make sense, and electricity didn't.

The only part of school he liked was Nature. In Nature, each student got one assignment for the year. You were supposed to observe a certain thing and write down everything you could about it. For instance, last year Kenny's assignment was Ants. He spent hours watching ants marching along in long wavery lines; he watched ants carrying bits of grass; he found the ant nest and figured out that the little white grainy things were ant eggs. He wrote it all down, added a few sketches, and his report was put with the collection in the schoolroom. The year before, his assignment was Blue Bird with Pointed Cap. That was harder, because birds were harder to follow around than ants. And another year, he did Strawberry Plant, and wrote about when to plant these plants, how they grew, and how hard it was to keep Blue Bird with Pointed Cap from stealing them.

The amazing thing was that Doon had done sort of the same thing back in his underground city. This was one reason Kenny felt so close to Doon—they were alike, at least in some ways. Doon had had a collection of insects that he observed and wrote about— but he'd had to leave it behind when he left. Kenny wished he could have seen it. He thought probably it was a masterpiece.

Other than Nature, school seemed confusing or boring to Kenny. He'd learned to read a long time ago, but he didn't much like doing it. There wasn't anything very interesting to read. And he'd learned his numbers well enough, up to the part where you have one number on top of another one, with a line between them. He got a little lost after that.

He was restless in school. The outside called to him, even in winter. On days when it wasn't raining, and when his mother didn't need him to help with some household task, he went down to the rain-swollen river and watched the water pour over the rocks, or he went up into the woods on the other side and poked around, happy if he could spot an owl having its daytime sleep or a rabbit disappearing into the grass.

One cold afternoon, he put on two sweaters and a jacket and went looking for Doon. Doon was a kind of cross between big brother and hero to Kenny. He hadn't seen him since the day after the roamer came, when he'd taught him how to make a whistle. It would be good to talk to him, Kenny thought, so he took off down the river road toward the Pioneer Hotel.

The air was icy, but the sun was out, and Kenny moved along at an easy lope. He passed the Ark, where people were working to patch the broken roof, and farther on, he passed some people combing through a thicket of withered brown blackberry bushes, looking for the tiny dried-up berries that the birds sometimes missed. He thought he would like to have some of those berries right now—just thinking about them made him feel the empty spot in his stomach—but when he asked if they'd found any, the searchers said they hadn't.

When he arrived at the Pioneer, Kenny went around to the back to see what was going on. People were at work destroying old buildings out in the churned-up field. Stacks of boards stood everywhere, and windows in their frames leaned against each other, and chunks of concrete and stones were heaped in mounds like small hills. When spring came and the weather was more reliable, these materials would be used, along with mud-and-straw bricks, to build the houses so badly needed by the people still living in the decrepit hotel.

Kenny trotted around, looking for Doon. He didn't see him. Sadge Merrill was out there, lugging a big heavy beam across the sodden ground, his breath puffing clouds into the air. The boy named Chet Noam was there carrying buckets of nails, and even the fragile little Miss Thorn, who had been a teacher in Ember, was out there wearing overalls and a big quilted coat, helping to lay string along the ground to mark the outlines of the future houses. Kenny wandered around, watching all this, and finally he saw Doon's father over by the hotel's back door. A big tub of nails and bolts and washers and things was beside him, and he was sorting those things into piles with his left hand. His right hand was all bandaged up.

Kenny went up to him. "Hi, Doon's father," he said.

"Hi, Kenny." Loris Harrow looked up from his work and smiled.

"What happened to your hand?" Kenny asked.

Doon's father explained.

"Is it better?" Kenny asked.

"I think so," said Doon's father. "It feels a little . . . well, a little sore and swollen, but I guess that's to be expected."

"I'm looking for Doon," Kenny said. "I can't find him."

"That's because he isn't here," said Doon's father. "He's staying up at Doctor Hester's house this week, helping out. He left yesterday."

So Kenny turned around and started up the river road again, heading for the other end of the village. He moved along idly, stopping to observe a beetle lying on its back with its legs waving (he turned it over with a twig), and to pick up a blue feather that wasn't too muddy, and to pitch a rock as far as he could throw it out into the field. He saw a few people down by the river. They had poles with them; they'd be hoping to catch fish.

By the time Kenny got to the doctor's house, it was late afternoon. In the courtyard, Torren was sitting on a bench in a patch of sunlight. He was playing with one of his treasures, a toy airplane, making it climb and dive in the air. Poppy stood by his knee, breaking a twig into pieces. She was so bundled up that she looked like a small puffy package with feet.

"Hi, Torren," Kenny said. "Is Doon here?"

"No. Why would he be? He's probably down working at the Pioneer the way he always is."

"Nope," said Kenny. "I looked for him there. Where's Lina?"

"She's down there, too," Torren said. "They needed some extra help, so she went. For three or four days. I think she was tired of being here and wanted a big change. Maddy came up to stay with us. She's in the kitchen making soup."

"Oh," said Kenny. He thought about this. He could tell that someone had the facts wrong, but he wasn't sure who.

Poppy pulled on his sleeve. "I breaked the stick," she said.

"You did," said Kenny. "Good girl." He patted Poppy's head. "How long has Lina been gone?"

"I don't know." Torren sent his airplane into a steep dive. "Just a couple of days, I think. Why?"

"Oh, nothing. I just wondered why . . . I just think it's kind of strange that . . . Oh, well. Never mind. I have to get going now."

"Going where?" said Torren, putting his airplane down. "And what's strange?"

The door of the house opened just then, and Mrs. Murdo came out. There were stains on her shirt, and her hair straggled. Kenny could tell she was tired. "Hello, Kenny," she said. "Poppy, it's much too cold for you to be outside. Time for you to come in. You, too, Torren."

"I'm not cold," Torren said.

Mrs. Murdo shrugged. It was clear she was not up to arguing with him. "Come in when you are, then," she said. She took Poppy's hand, and they went back into the house.

"So I'm going," said Kenny. "Bye."

"But where are you going?"

"Nowhere. Just back into town."

"Can I come with you? You can tell me what's strange."

"No," Kenny said. He wished he hadn't said a thing about it. "I'm just going home. I can't be late for dinner."

"No one ever tells me anything," said Torren. He glowered at Kenny, but Kenny ignored him and went back out to the road.

He puzzled over what he'd heard as he walked

toward town. Doon's father thought Doon was at the doctor's house, but he wasn't. Torren thought Lina was at the Pioneer, but as far as Kenny could tell, she wasn't. What did this mean? He concentrated hard on figuring it out and did not hear the steps behind him.

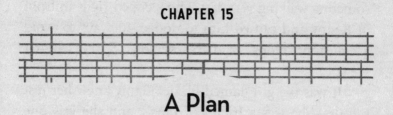

CHAPTER 15

A Plan

Evening was coming on now. Kenny's ears ached from the cold. He picked up his pace. By the time he got to the main plaza, he had worked things out in his mind: Doon and Lina weren't where they usually were; they weren't where they'd said they were going to be, either. No one seemed worried about this, so that meant Doon's father and Mrs. Murdo hadn't happened to talk to each other lately. And that meant that Kenny was now the only person who knew this secret.

So the question was, he thought as he crossed the plaza, where most of the shops were closed and only a few people hurried toward home, should he tell anyone that Lina and Doon were missing? Probably he should, but then, on the other hand, it was clear that they were missing on purpose. Maybe he shouldn't give away their secret? Or not yet anyhow?

From around the corner by the town hall came

someone walking very fast who stepped right in front of Kenny and caused him to dodge sideways to avoid a collision. "Oops," said this person. "Sorry, I didn't see you."

It was the girl named Lizzie. Kenny knew her just a little—she was a friend of Lina's, and she was one of the few people he'd ever seen who had hair the color of apricots, though right now, her hair didn't shine the way it had in the summer, and her face was pale, almost bluish.

"Oh, it's you," Lizzie said.

"I heard you were sick," said Kenny. "Are you better?"

"I am," Lizzie answered, "but I *almost* died of it. I coughed so hard I cracked one of my ribs. I thought I was going to cough my lungs right up out of my chest." She looked at him rather proudly.

"That's too bad," said Kenny. He was thinking. Should he tell Lizzie about Lina and Doon? It felt wrong to tell Doon's father and Mrs. Murdo, who would be upset and alarmed; that felt like a betrayal of whatever Doon and Lina's plan was. But it was hard to keep the secret all to himself. He needed someone to talk it over with, someone he could trust. Could he trust Lizzie? He knew she'd been the girl-friend of that boy named Tick, who had deceived them all. But it wasn't her fault she'd been deceived by him; everyone had.

Lizzie turned to go. Kenny hesitated another second, and then he said, "Have you seen Lina lately?"

"No," said Lizzie. She looked into the air, thinking. "I haven't seen her since . . . it must have been three or four days ago. Why?"

"Well, listen," Kenny said. He took hold of Lizzie's scarf and pulled her around the corner, where the wall kept them out of the wind. "Here's what I just found out."

As he explained the mystery, Lizzie listened with avid interest. So did Torren, who was hiding behind the stump of the tree that had burned last summer. He had decided he was sick and tired of being left behind and sick and tired of being left out of secrets, and he'd followed Kenny into town and ducked into his hiding place when Kenny ran into Lizzie. He thought the mystery of Lina and Doon was not only interesting but also infuriating. Once again, people had gone off on some kind of adventure without including him. It made him so mad that he couldn't keep quiet.

"I bet *I* know where they went!" he cried, jumping out from behind the tree stump and nearly scaring Kenny and Lizzie out of their skins.

"You followed me," said Kenny.

Torren ignored this. "We have to find them," he said. "I can help."

"It's no use," said Lizzie. "They have run away

together." She took hold of her hair and stuffed it down into her collar to keep the wind from blowing it around. "I always knew they liked each other in a special way. You could just tell."

"Where would they go?" Kenny asked.

"Someplace cozy," Lizzie said. "Where they could set things up like a real home. It would be so much fun," she said wistfully.

"But they're only thirteen," said Kenny.

"That doesn't matter. This is a whole new world! The rules aren't the same."

"You are being dumb," Torren said. "That is *not* what Lina would do. I know that. She wouldn't leave Poppy just to go off with Doon. I know she wouldn't."

"You're too young to understand," said Lizzie.

"I am not." Torren glared at her. "I know what they did," he said. "They were sick of being cold and not having enough to eat. So they went off to be roamers, to go someplace else and get away from everything. I bet someone in town has a wagon missing, and an ox. I bet they went toward the old city, because Lina knew the way from when she went before."

Kenny listened to these ideas without saying anything much. Possible, but not right, he thought. Even though Torren lived in the same house as Lina, and Lizzie had known both Lina and Doon in Ember, neither one seemed really to know them very well.

Lizzie and Torren argued back and forth. Lizzie said again that Torren was too young to understand and talked about someone named Looper back in Ember that she would have gone off with if he'd asked her to, and Torren said that *anybody* would want to be a roamer if they could, even if they had to steal a wagon to do it, and that his brother Caspar was a roamer and that when he was old enough, he and Caspar would be a team.

Finally, Lizzie turned to Kenny. "You're not saying anything," she said. "Who do you think is right, me or him?"

"Well, I think neither one," said Kenny. "What I think is, they wanted to be helpful. There's hardship here, just the way there was hardship in their city before, and they wanted to help then."

Lizzie and Torren both stared at him and said nothing for a moment. Then Lizzie said, "You might be right."

"Might be," said Torren.

"So if they wanted to help," Lizzie went on, "where would they go?"

"Someplace where they could find things we don't have."

"But where is that? No one around here has anything."

Kenny looked up at the sky, thinking. He rubbed

his chin. If *he* wanted to help, what would he do? Where would he go? "Maybe up north?" he said. "Maybe they caught a ride with that roamer who was here."

"But once they got there, how could they buy things?" said Lizzie. "They had nothing to trade with."

"That's true."

Lizzie frowned, thinking. "Maybe the ancient ruined city? Maybe when Lina went there, she saw things that were still left."

"No," said Torren, "if there'd been good things still there, Caspar would have brought them back."

They were stumped. They stood there in the cold alley, their ears and tips of their noses getting more and more chilly. Lizzie wound her scarf around her head. She coughed. "It's so much *colder* here than it was in Ember," she complained. "And the air here isn't just cold, it *moves* and slices into you, which makes it worse." She coughed again, a raspy cough that made her eyes water. "And in Ember," she went on, "no water or ice falls out of the sky the way it does here, and even though people got sick there, at least they had medicine that sometimes helped a little bit. In Ember . . ." She stopped. "Oh," she said.

"Oh, what?" said Torren.

"I think I know where they went," said Lizzie.

"To Ember!" Kenny cried. "I bet you're right! But is anything left there?"

"Might be," said Lizzie. "At least a little bit. Probably more than here."

"Then that's it. That's where they went." Kenny felt sure of it. It felt right for both Lina and Doon: they wanted to help, they knew their old city, and they were brave enough to try to go there on their own.

"So what should we do?" Lizzie said. "Go after them and tell them it's too dangerous, and they should come back?"

"*Is* it dangerous?" Kenny asked.

"It must be," Lizzie said. "It's dark there now. And how would they even get in? They couldn't go up that river." She swiped at her runny nose. "I think their minds must have got a little bit unhinged by the cold and the trouble here and everything."

"We should rescue them!" cried Torren. "I don't mind going out into the wilderness. It will be good practice for when I'm a roamer."

"But we don't know the way," said Kenny.

"I could remember it, maybe," Lizzie said. "It's up there." She waved her hand in a vague northeasterly direction.

"We can't catch up with them," Kenny said. "They've been gone too long. Maybe they're already on their way back. Or maybe they've had an accident and they're stuck out there. If we went up on the hill beyond the far field, we might see them. Then we could go and help."

Torren was jumping up and down by now, his eyes shining and coat flapping. "We have to go *soon*!" he cried.

"But not in the night." Lizzie wrapped her jacket closer around her.

"Tomorrow," said Kenny. "We could meet at the far field early, right at sunrise. Okay? We'll just go up and look."

"Okay!" cried Torren. "We'll go tomorrow!" He jumped up and thumped the wall with his fist. A few yards away, a window was pushed open, and in a moment Ben Barlow poked his head out. "What's all that commotion?" he called, but no one was there.

CHAPTER 16

A Night with Maggs

"All right," said Maggs. "Now I'll show you where I got that book." She had dropped Lina's picture message from the cliff and come back. The sky was growing rapidly darker, as the sun was setting and the rain clouds rising, so Maggs unhooked a lantern from the side of her wagon. It was a tin-can lantern with a candle burning inside, much like the lanterns used in Sparks. "Follow me," she said. She headed for the grove of trees to the left of the cave entrance, the place where Lina had gathered kindling the night before. They went in among the thickets of brush and stickery branches. "It was in here somewhere," Maggs said, stomping through the undergrowth. "I wasn't the one who found it—that was Wash—but he showed it to the rest of us afterward."

It was dark among the trees; not much light from the sky filtered through. Maggs's lantern made a spot of gold ahead of Lina, and she went fast to keep up with it. After a few minutes, the ground rose slightly uphill. Maggs edged between the thickly growing tree trunks, and Lina followed, her feet swishing through deep layers of leaves.

"Here we go," said Maggs. Lina came up behind her and saw what she'd glimpsed before: a faint reflection glinting through the woods ahead. "Now, watch your step," said Maggs. "We're close."

A moment later, Maggs cried, "Ouch!" and stopped so abruptly that Lina almost bumped into her. "Stubbed my toe," Maggs grumped. She kicked away some leaves, and beneath them Lina saw a step— square-cornered, smooth, clearly man-made. And just beyond the step, the light glinted on metal. She stared in amazement. There was a door in the mountainside. It had a metal handle, and a metal border ran along its edges.

The door swung open with a creak when Maggs pulled on its handle. "There might be bats or animals in here," Maggs said. "You better let me go in first." She stepped inside. "No bats, no animals," she announced. So Lina followed her in. The lantern showed them a plain, windowless room, completely empty except for a small metal table that lay on its side on the floor. A few leaves, no doubt blown in by the wind, were scattered near the threshold. That was all.

"The book was in here?" said Lina. "There wasn't anything else in the room?"

"Oh, yes," said Maggs. "There was the jewel. Wash took that, of course. He gave me the book for starting fires."

"The jewel?" Lina asked. "What was the jewel?"

"A diamond," Maggs said. "That's what Wash said it was. Just like in that song I sang you. Beautiful thing. He'll be able to get a good price for it someday."

Lina was mystified and disappointed. The book must be about the jewel. But why would you need a book about a jewel? Jewels were just for decoration. Anyhow, the jewel was gone. There wouldn't be much to tell Doon after all.

"Well, thanks for showing me," Lina said.

"You're welcome," said Maggs. "Now we need to get back to my wagon and get going if we're going to make any progress at all before dark."

They didn't make much progress. They walked for half an hour or so, and then the light was entirely gone from the sky. "Time to set up camp," Maggs said. "Over there looks like a good place."

Herding the sheep with shouts and pokes, she headed for a clump of low-spreading oak trees, and when the wagon was under their branches, she halted the horse that was towing it and unhooked his harness.

"What's that horse's name?" Lina asked.

"Happy," said Maggs.

"He doesn't look happy," Lina said.

"Well, he used to be. He's old, and it's hard to be happy when you're old."

Lina wondered if this was true. She thought not. Her granny had been old, and she was usually happy. If this horse had enough to eat and didn't have to work so hard, she'd bet he'd be happy, too. She gave his bony flank a pat.

"We'll make our fire right here," Maggs said, hacking at the ground with the heel of one boot. "Better do it quick, before the rain comes. Get some kindling."

Lina scurried around, gathering up grass and twigs and branches and carrying it all to Maggs. Soon Maggs had built a sturdy stack, with the kindling on the bottom and bigger sticks on top. "Now to get a flame," she said. She took a couple of stones out of a little pouch attached to her belt.

"Wait," said Lina. "I have a match." She took off her pack, reached inside, and pulled out a match.

Maggs looked at it greedily. "How many have you got?" she asked. "I used up the one I got from you."

"I only have a few left," Lina answered. She was determined to guard them carefully. She'd practiced using flintstones to make a spark, but she wasn't very good at it. She didn't want to be left without matches.

Even with a match, it was hard to get the fire going. The grass was damp from the rains of winter, and even when the flame caught, the wind kept blowing it out. Lina used up two more matches relighting it. "I should never have sold that book," Maggs said. "We could use it right now."

"It's terrible to burn a book," said Lina. "You never know what might be in it."

Maggs just said "Pfft," and shook her head.

Finally, the fire burned more strongly. "Now," said Maggs. "You watch it. I'll get the wagon ready. We're both going to have to cram inside tonight."

She disappeared into the wagon again. It shook and rattled, and a pot, a skillet, a couple of tin boxes, and a big bucket all came flying from its rear end. "I'll have to take more out later," Maggs said when she emerged. "It's pretty crowded in there."

"It's very . . . unusual," Lina said. "The wagon cover, I mean. So many colors."

"Like it?" the roamer said. "I made it myself. It's all pieces of old plastic and tin—bags, raincoats, umbrellas, flat cans, stuff like that. Been collecting it for years."

They had some sort of gluey soup for dinner, slightly warmed up over the fire and drunk out of cracked cups. Maggs slurped hers noisily, and she talked as she slurped. For the next half hour or so, as they sat there by their small, sputtering fire, she hardly stopped talking at all. Mostly she talked about her hardships. It was hard to find people who'd give you more than five sacks of corn for a sheep; it was hard to keep slogging back and forth between this mountain and the various miserable settlements around here; it was hard to control the sheep—if they wandered off, wolves could get them; it was hard to be out here in the winter weather, trying to find some old barn or abandoned house to take shelter in. "That last big thunderstorm that came through nearly killed me," she said. "I found an old stable to stay in, but water came in through the roof and put my fire out, and lightning hit a tree right next to the stable and burned it to the ground." She shook her stick at the sky, as if threatening whoever was up there making the weather. "I am a kind and generous person and a devoted sister," she said, "but enough is enough."

At that moment, something called through the darkness—a long note that soared upward, fell and faded, and soared up again. Lina turned her head quickly. "What's that?"

"Wolves," said Maggs. "Getting ready to hunt."

"I've never seen a wolf," said Lina.

"Well, lucky you," Maggs said. "It's a good idea to stay away from them. Have you seen that green star? The one that moves?"

"Yes," Lina said.

"That's a weird one," said Maggs. "Never stays in the same place, like a normal star. Disappears for days on end, then comes back, moves around, acts all wrong."

"But it isn't dangerous, is it?" asked Lina. Maybe she should add it to her list of terrible things.

"Who knows?" Maggs drained her cup and wiped it out with the tail of her shirt. "Might be, might not be."

Clouds had blotted out the stars by now, and the wind was flinging down the first drops of rain. The sheep, which had been wandering and munching in a loose group, began huddling together, and soon they stood right up against each other, forming a big woolly mass. "Got to get a new dog," said Maggs, frowning at them.

"A dog?" Lina said. "Why?"

"A dog would warn me if wolves were around. It would scare them off and protect the sheep. My old dog got bitten by a rattlesnake a couple of months ago, and I haven't found a good replacement yet."

Lina added rattlesnakes to her list of dangers. "Do you know how to make a wolf-scaring whistle?" she asked. "With a grass blade?"

"Oh, yes," Maggs said. "That helps sometimes." She pulled a stubby candle from one of the many bags tied onto her belt and lit it from the fire. "Take this and climb in there," she said, pointing to the wagon. "Quick, before you get wet."

Lina took the candle in one hand and her pack in the other. She went over to the wagon's rear opening. She pushed aside a flap of the patchy cover and put one knee on the wagon and hoisted herself up. It was hard to do, holding the candle, but she managed it. She pushed her pack in and crept inside.

Ick. What a place. It was low and small and crowded and smelled like sheep sweat or sheep breath or something to do with sheep, and there didn't seem room in it for even one person, much less two. Stuff hung from hooks overhead and was packed in wads on the floor and against the sides, and her candle made shadows behind every lump, in every cranny, next to every shelf and sack and bunched-up rag of clothing. Lina's heart sank. But she heard the pattering of rain on the wagon's tent, and she thought about how it would be to walk across the hills in the dark with the rain pounding down on her face and soaking her clothes. This is better, she thought. It's awful, but it's better.

There were two more or less flat surfaces, which she guessed were where they would sleep. Basically, they were benches with blankets and other stuff piled on them. They were right next to each other along the length of the wagon, with only a few inches between. She'd be sleeping very close to Maggs, who had a powerful smell and might have bugs crawling on her. But there was no way around it.

Lina spotted a small can with wax drippings on its sides. She stuck the candle in it to free up her hands.

The wagon gave a lurch, and she staggered sideways and fell onto one of the benches. Maggs's shaggy head appeared at the rear. "That's right!" she shouted. "That one's yours. Rain is here! I'm coming in."

At first there really wasn't room for both of them at all. Lina scrunched up her knees, and Maggs banged around, shifting and shoving things, and stuff clattered down from hooks and shelves and bumped into Lina's head, and Maggs grumbled and muttered, and the rain spattered ever harder on the canvas roof.

"Some of this stuff," Maggs said, "I can just pitch out." She tossed a soup pot and a water bottle out into the night, and then a dishpan and some rubber boots and a broken three-legged stool. "Might need these tonight, though. I'll keep them close." She reached up and tugged on something, and suddenly a flock of tin cans cascaded onto her head with a terrific clatter. Maggs didn't seem bothered. She lifted an arm, and Lina saw that the cans were all strung together in a bunch. "What's that?" she asked.

"It's to scare off wolves," Maggs said. She shook

the bunch, and the violent clatter sounded again. "I made it myself. If we hear any wolf noises in the night, we just go out and shake these around. Usually works."

It was a long and very uncomfortable night. The wind rocked the wagon, and drips of rain crept in through the seams of the canvas tent. Maggs snored and groaned and thrashed around, jabbing Lina with an elbow now and then and breathing rotten onion breath. Lina pressed as far from her as she could, up against the side of the wagon, and closed her eyes. But there was no peaceful darkness inside her mind. She was haunted by visions: Doon hauled away by kidnappers; Ember smoke-filled and firelit; dreadful strangers with flames on their heads; and the angry faces she expected to see when she got back to Sparks, having caused more trouble than the town already had.

That same night, Kenny and Lizzie and Torren were also having trouble sleeping. They were listening unhappily to the rain. What if it didn't stop by morning? What if they couldn't go on their rescue adventure? All three of them really, really wanted to.

And down in Ember, in the lair of the Troggs, Doon wasn't even trying to sleep. He was thinking as hard as he could, putting together in his mind everything he'd seen and heard during the day, everything that might give him a clue about how to free himself. Finally, a possibility came to him. If he was wrong, he'd be in even worse trouble than now. But he thought he might be right. His heart started up a fast and steady thudding.

CHAPTER 17

The Secret of the Key

Doon waited until Trogg's snore was steady, Scawgo had stopped whimpering, and everyone seemed soundly asleep. He sat up. Holding on to the chain so it wouldn't make a noise, he swung his legs off the side of the couch. He took off his shirt and then his undershirt, which was made of old, soft, limp cotton, and he wrapped the undershirt around the chain, stuffing it into the cuffs around each of his ankles. Cautiously, he moved one foot just an inch. No clink. He put his shirt and jacket on, stuffed his scarf in his pocket, and stood up. He took his lightcap from the floor, folded it around the candle, and put it in his other pocket. Then, with one tiny awkward step at a time, in total darkness except for the faint glow in the window from the low fire down in Harken Square, he moved toward the door.

There he paused. All was silent, except for sounds

of breathing and snoring. No one had heard him. He thought of the diamond in the closet. He had the strong feeling that the diamond was like a child stolen from its rightful parent—it needed to be rescued, and he was the one who should do it. The risk would be tremendous. If they heard him and stopped him, his chance for freedom might never come again. He had told Trogg that he was not a thief. But the diamond was *meant* for the people of Ember; he was sure it was. So really it was Trogg who'd stolen it. Should he try to get it, right now? He could hardly bear the thought of leaving it behind. But if he tried for it and was caught and lost his chance for freedom . . . then what? Standing there in the dark, he weighed these questions for several seconds. He chose freedom, finally. But in the back of his mind, he held on to a hope that he might return somehow and get another chance at the treasure that should be his.

He turned the knob of the apartment door. It opened soundlessly. He went out and shut the door behind him. He sat down on the top step and then, one soft silent bump at a time, he went down the stairs on his seat. At the bottom, he paused again within the shadow of the doorway, looking out into the square.

There was Minny, sitting with her back to him in a big armchair by the fire with a stack of short sticks by her side and one long stick in her hand. She gave the fire a poke and a few sparks flew up. Then she sat for a while without moving. Doon waited. Some minutes later, she reached down for a chunk of wood and tossed it on the fire. The flames caught it and danced a little brighter. Doon leaned against the stairway wall, determined to wait as long as it might take.

It wasn't too long. After ten minutes or so, Minny's head began to dip. It dipped down and jerked up, dipped again, jerked up. Finally, she lost the struggle. Her chin sank toward her chest; Doon saw the curve of her bony neck. Then she began to snore: a weak, sniveling snore, a sort of bubbly whine.

Now. Doon stepped out onto the pavement. He made his way toward Minny, inch by inch. It took a long time. Once, she stopped snoring and sat up. Doon froze. But she only poked the fire feebly and slumped down again.

Beside the fire, a few yards from her chair, the forks and knives and pots and pans from last night's dinner lay scattered on the ground. Barely breathing, Doon crept up to them. He chose the smallest knife. He slid it away from anything it might clank against and picked it up with two fingers. Then he moved on toward Minny.

Another dozen microscopic steps. He had to stop once to tuck the undershirt back around the chain when it began to come loose. Finally, he was standing behind her. Now. If his guess was right, this was the moment when he would know.

It was her nervousness that had given him the clue—especially the way she had an attack of it every time she came near him. He had noticed that her hand fluttered up to her throat, that she clutched her chest, that she skittered away from him. Was it because she had the key?

The dim firelight glinted faintly on the knob of greasy hair at the top of Minny's head. Doon bent as close as he dared, holding his breath, peering at her bare, scrawny neck. His heart leapt—right so far. Against the tendons of her neck lay a string. In one swift motion, he lifted the string from her skin, cut it, and pulled it away. And yes—there was the key.

Minny stirred. She slapped at her neck and muttered. Doon, gripping the key, took a step back. If Minny woke now and saw him, it was all over.

But she slumped again and resumed her snoring. Doon backed up a few more steps, then bent over and fitted the key into the lock that held his chain. The lock opened; he unwrapped his shirt from the chain and pulled the chain, one careful link at a time, from the ankle cuffs.

Just as he was straightening up to run, a chunk of wood in the fire dropped with a thump and a sizzle of sparks. That was the sound that brought Minny awake. She sat up. She groped for her stick. Doon, standing only a few feet behind her, froze. If he moved now, she would turn around and see him.

With her stick in her hand, Minny stood up and took a step toward the fire. At the same time, with great caution, Doon took a step backward. Minny pushed at the fire, moving the embers around, and as she did, Doon stepped back farther. He had to reach the buildings and get out of sight—hide himself in a doorway before Minny turned and stay there until she fell asleep again.

He thought he had managed it. He'd gone far enough to feel a wall at his back when she turned away from the fire, and she didn't look up as she went toward her chair and sank into it. Doon got ready to run. He'd go back to Greystone Street to pick up his pack, and then he'd head for the path that led up and out. His legs itched to get going.

Then Minny, having done her fire-watch duty, seemed to recall her other duty. She raised a hand and patted her neck. She straightened up. She patted more quickly. She scrabbled at her neck with her fingers, pushing her hands under her collar and slapping at her chest. With a low moan, she sprang to her feet. Frantically, she peered at the ground around her chair. When she spotted the dropped chain behind it, she let out a piercing wail. "Oh, help, help!" she cried. "He's stolen the key! He's escaping!" She grabbed a couple of pans and clanged them together. *Bang! Bang!* The Troggs would be jumping from their beds. Before

Doon could form a thought, he heard their thumps and voices overhead.

Running was impossible. He'd be seen and chased. So he ducked into the nearest doorway—the one next to the Troggs' apartment—and pressed himself back into the shadows and held still.

It was no more than a minute before all three Troggs thundered down the steps and out into Harken Square. They'd thrown coats on over their nightshirts, and their shoes were unfastened. Yorick was in the lead. His hair stood up crazily. "Which way did he go?" he yelled at Minny.

"We know which way, dunderhead!" Trogg shouted. "He's heading for the exit. Fan out, all of you. You, too, Minny. We'll all go toward the path but take different streets. When you see him, give a shout." He turned back toward the building. Doon flinched, but Trogg wasn't looking in his direction. "Scawgo!" he shouted. "Get down here and mind the fire!" Then the four of them raced away.

Doon took a long breath. He would have to find his pack and then hide somewhere until the Troggs gave up their search. That might take a long time. Disappointment drained his energy. He had wanted so badly to get out *now*.

Overhead, he heard a sound—a scrape, then a pause, then a scrape and a thump. A moment later, uneven footsteps on the stairs next door: *ka-bump, ka-bump.* Doon peered from his doorway and saw Scawgo come out into the square.

"Doon!" Scawgo whispered.

"I'm here," Doon whispered back.

Scawgo limped over to him, going as fast as he could, carrying something. "I heard you get up," Scawgo said breathlessly, "and I watched you from the window. Then she yelled and they all left, and the house was empty, so I got you this." He handed Doon a small yellow-wrapped bundle. "Take it, quick."

Doon's heart leapt. He knew what this was. But he hesitated. "You'll get in trouble," he said.

"No, I won't," said Scawgo. "He'll think *you* took it." He smiled and handed Doon the bundle. "Thank you for getting my treasures," he said.

Doon laid a hand briefly on Scawgo's shoulder. "I'll be back for you." Then at last he ran.

At top speed, with the metal cuffs bouncing and scraping against his ankles, he ran up Gilly Street, around the corner onto Rockbellow Road, and into the deep shadow at the back of the Gathering Hall. Light from the fire shone faintly along the side streets, just enough to keep him oriented. First of all, he must find his pack—he had to have his generator, left behind when he was captured. He moved as quickly as he dared in the darkness, keeping his mind focused on exactly where he was. He drew his hand along the wall beside him; he counted the doorways. When he got to where he thought he'd left his pack, he swept his foot around in all directions, and at last he bumped against it. He grabbed it up, put the bundle Scawgo had given him inside, and slung the pack onto his back.

His hands were sweating, and his heart was going so fast it was more like a rattle than a beat. He gave himself a moment to think. He couldn't go toward the path, because the Troggs would ambush him there. He'd have to wait for them to leave before he could get out of the city. But it occurred to him that he didn't have to waste that time hunkering down in a dark apartment. There was something much more useful he could do. He would head for the Pipeworks.

CHAPTER 18

In the Pipeworks

When he got to the Pipeworks, its door stood partly open. Doon stepped inside and was instantly met by the smell of old rubber and mold, so familiar that it swept him backward in time. Everything looked the same as it had when he'd last been here—the slickers hanging on their hooks, the boots tumbled below—and he remembered his first day as a Pipeworks laborer and how determined he had been to discover the secret of the generator and save the city by fixing it. The generator had been past hope by then, on its way to the complete death it was close to now. The way out of Ember had turned out to be very different from what he'd expected.

Lighting his way with his own small generator, he started down the long stairway that led to the underground river. Even with the light from the bulb, the narrow steps were hard to see, and he had to go slowly and place his feet with care so as not to slip. He couldn't help thinking, with a shudder, of the people who had died here. He was actually grateful that Trogg had "cleaned them up." It would have been dreadful to come upon them himself.

It seemed a long time before he came out on the walkway beside the river. But when at last he did, the river's sound was the same as always—a thunderous churning as the water rushed between the stone banks, rising from the north end of the Pipeworks and streaming away through the great mouthlike opening at the south end, the hole he and Lina had sped through in their little boat.

Doon paused by the river and tried to bring up the map of the Pipeworks in his mind. He needed to picture the way to get through the maze of tunnels to that room where he'd found the mayor asleep amid the piles and piles of things he had stolen from the people of Ember.

But the Pipeworks was a different place now. The blackness beyond Doon's light, the roar of the unseeable river, and the sense of an endless emptiness in the twisting passageways—this was no longer the busy hive of activity it had been when he worked here. No human presence remained, except perhaps for the ghosts of those who'd been lost in the tunnels long ago or drowned in the river during the mad rush from the city.

He took the third tunnel to the left off the main path by the river. Now, Doon told himself, I need the fourth opening in the right-hand wall. He made his way along. His generator made a bright circle, lighting the front of his jacket and the tops of his shoes and the walls to either side of him. But he couldn't see more than a few feet ahead, which threw off his sense of distance.

The pipes that ran along the walls and the ceiling were now, after nine months of neglect, in even worse shape than they had been. Water seeped down the walls and dripped from the ceiling; every so often, his feet plunged into a puddle, and the water splashed up onto his legs. He began to feel unsure if he'd passed two tunnel entrances or three; he couldn't get a sense of the length of the passage he was in and how far he'd gone. When he came to what he thought was the fourth opening, he hesitated. What if he'd taken a wrong turn or missed an opening without realizing it?

But his memory had not failed him. Minutes later, he went around a curve and there it was: the tunnel that had been roped off when he first came across it. The rope was still there, but now one end of it was loose and lay on the ground, and when he went down the passage, he found that the door at the end stood open. He stepped inside.

And smiled.

He had meant to leave the Pipeworks after checking the mayor's room. But just as he came to the main pathway beside the river, the city took another of its shuddering breaths. Doon heard the grinding and squealing of the ancient generator as its wheels and cranks started up, and overhead the lights blinked and came on. For a moment, everything looked as it used to. The main tunnel stretched in both directions, with the dark hollows of the smaller tunnels along it. On the rippling, rushing surface of the water, splinters of light glinted like darting fish.

Doon stood on the riverbank, looking, remembering, and thinking. He came to a decision he knew was right.

Quickly, before the lights could fade again, he ran along the riverwalk to the generator room. The one time he'd been in here before, the noise and confusion had been so overwhelming that he'd stayed only a few moments. Now he wasted no time gazing at the monstrous old machine. The first thing he did was kick through the litter of rusty old parts and abandoned tools lying on the floor until he found a screwdriver, which he thrust into his pocket. Then he set down his own small generator and made right for the place where an arm of the great machine plunged into the river.

He had to crawl on his knees into a narrow space between the whirring gears and the edge of the riverbank to get at it. A stout pipe, mottled with scum and rust, emerged from the generator's side, made a right-angle turn, and went straight down into the water. Where it entered, Doon could see something vast and dark and iron-looking under the surface, turning in halting jolts. It was the wheel that somehow caused the generator to create electricity.

He would have to break off that pipe—to disconnect the power of the river from the machine. He darted back to where the tools lay scattered and found a wrench that would do. Using his old Pipeworks skills, which came back to him readily, he tightened the wrench around the joint of the connecting pipe and hauled at it as hard as he could. He nearly fell backward into the river. The pipe was so old and rotten that it came apart, crumbling into rough-edged flakes, and right away the gears of the generator slowed and the light began to fade. In a moment, Doon stood in total darkness.

The only sound was the rush of the river. No more water would be pumped up into the city, and the lights were gone for good. Before too long, the Troggs would have to leave, which was as it should be. They didn't belong in Ember. And yet Doon felt a swell of sorrow. He had killed his city. He felt the pain of it right in the center of himself, as if someone he loved had died. It was true, he thought. He had loved Ember, with all its problems. But Ember's time was over.

* * *

Now he faced a dilemma. The Troggs were waiting for him by the exit path, determined not to let him get out and spread the word about their private underground kingdom. He wouldn't be able to get past them without being seen. Even if he did, he couldn't go up without a light, and they'd see the light. He had to keep them from following him.

And he was pretty sure he knew how to do it. He groped his way across the generator room, found his own generator by the door, and cranked its handle. By its light, he made his way back down the riverside path and started up the stairway. When he was nearly to the top, he took a fresh candle from his pack, lit it, and dripped some of its wax onto the step. He stuck the candle in the melted wax, sat down on the step next to it, and took the screwdriver from his pocket. By the candle's light, he undid the ankle cuffs that Trogg had fastened onto him. He gave his legs a quick rub. It felt great not to have the metal banging his bones and chafing his skin. Then he left the candle there—it would burn for an hour—and climbed the rest of the stairs.

When he reached the locker room, he propped the door to the stairway open with a heavy bucket. He darted into the Pipeworks office and grabbed a key from a ring on the wall. Back in the locker room, he picked up a toolbox—the kind he used to use when he worked here, full of wrenches and hammers. He stepped outside onto the street and used the toolbox to prop the street door open, too.

Now came the tricky part. Cranking his generator just enough to light a few steps ahead, he made his way across Plummer Square to Liverie Street. This would lead him to the area where the Troggs were lying in wait, though he couldn't know exactly where they were. He stopped and stood still, listening. He heard no voices, no footsteps. With his hand against the wall, he crept farther along. He had to be close to Blott Street now. This was far enough—he might run into one of them any moment.

Doon took a quick breath. Here goes, he thought.

He began to make the sound of running. He slapped his feet on the pavement, though he was not actually running but staying just where he was. He panted loudly.

"I hear him!" shouted Yorick from out of the darkness.

"He's over there!" shouted Kanza.

"Get him!" roared Trogg.

Doon gave a good loud yelp of fright. A few blocks ahead, he saw one of the Troggs (he couldn't tell which) come out of a doorway. He whirled around and ran, cranking his generator every few steps to keep his light going dimly, and when he got back to the Pipeworks door, he snatched up the toolbox and dumped its contents onto the street. The tools clanked and clattered.

He kicked most of them aside, as if hastily trying to hide them. Then, leaving the Pipeworks door open and giving the key a quick twist in the knob, he dashed back across the street and crept partway up the stairs beside a shop. He sat there, utterly still.

"The noise came from this way!" shouted the voice of Yorick.

"Come on, all you slowpokes! Faster!" That was Trogg.

Doon heard shoes slapping the pavement, and around the corner came the four headlights of the Troggs, joggling through the darkness.

"Here!" yelled Yorick, tripping over the scattered tools. "He dropped his weapons!"

"Wait, noodlehead," cried Trogg. "It's a trick! He wants us to think he's in there, and he's not!"

But Yorick had already dashed inside. "Wrong, Pa!" he shouted. "I see his light! He's on his way down those stairs!"

At that, the whole family rushed inside, Kanza yelling in glee, Minny scuttling along last. Doon, quick and silent, crossed the street and closed the Pipeworks door behind them. He had, of course, used the key to set the knob in the locked position. By the time the Troggs broke down the door to get out—there were plenty of hammers and wrenches in there to attack it with, but still it should take them at least an hour—he would be a good way up the path, out of their reach.

He made for Deeple Street. At the edge of the Unknown Regions, he exchanged his generator for a candle, which he fitted into his lightcap. Several minutes of fast walking brought him to the chasm, which he crossed with quick, careful steps, keeping his mind blank. On the other side, he gave the boards of the bridge a push so that they fell into the pit. Trogg could jump the pit, he knew, but still this might slow him down a little.

Like Lina, Doon noticed the cans and bottles that had been dropped to mark the way to the path. He followed their trail, going as fast as he could and aiming a hard kick at each one as he passed it, sending it skidding off into the darkness—another way to slow Trogg down. When he felt fatigue creeping up on him, he pictured the Troggs battering down the Pipeworks door, and that gave him the strength to keep going.

The climb up the path was arduous and long—he burned one candle after another on the way. But no one pursued him, as far as he could tell. He got safely to the top and edged through the crack to the outside. It was dark, but he could tell from the faintness of the stars that day was near.

He needed to rest, even for just a few minutes, before he could go on. But first he had to look at what Scawgo had given him. He took off his pack, felt inside it for the bundle, pulled it out, and unwound the yellow cloth. There was the diamond, glimmering in the dim light that was not yet dawn. He ran his hand over its glassy surface. He turned it upside down and saw twists and turns and tabs of metal within its circular collar. He didn't really know what this diamond was any more than Trogg did, and there was no time to examine it now—but he was sure he could find out. He felt grateful to Scawgo for giving it to him, even a bit grateful to Trogg for finding it in the first place. The diamond was meant to be his; through these unlikely people, it had come to him after all.

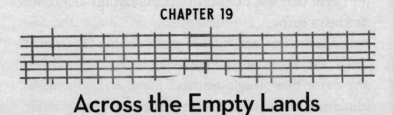

CHAPTER 19

Across the Empty Lands

Lina opened her eyes and remembered that she was in the wagon with Maggs the shepherd. The pattering of the rain had stopped, but it still seemed to be night. Quietly, she sat up and crept down the bench on her knees to look out the back. She could see a faint pink light at the line where the mountain met the sky. So it was almost morning.

Maggs was sleeping with her mouth hanging open and a string of drool on her chin. It would be a while before she could get moving, Lina knew. She didn't have time to wait.

She put on her jacket and picked up her pack, but it bumped against the side of the wagon as she was trying to get her arms into the straps. The wagon jolted, a plate fell off a shelf, and Maggs awoke.

"Watch out!" she shouted. "Robbers! Sheep burglars!" She sat up and conked her head on a tent beam.

"It's only me," Lina said. "I'm leaving. Thank you for helping me."

"You're leaving?" said Maggs, rubbing her head.

"Yes," Lina said. "I have to get home."

"Don't be in such a hurry," Maggs said. She wiped the drool from her chin with the corner of her blanket and looked around blearily. "I just need to get my clothes on, put a little breakfast together, round up the sheep, and feed the horse, and I'll be ready to go."

Lina shook her head. "I can't wait," she said. "I have to get home fast. I can walk faster than your wagon and your sheep can go."

"You can't go by yourself," said Maggs. "I'll go with you. There's wolves around."

"They won't bother me," Lina said.

"Don't be silly," said Maggs, yawning. "Get yourself some breakfast. I'll be up in a minute." She lay back down and pulled up her blanket.

"I don't need any breakfast," Lina said.

"Right over there," said Maggs as if she hadn't heard, waving a hand at some bags on the floor. "Carrots. Nuts. Dry sheep cheese." She closed her eyes and pulled a pillow over her head.

Lina opened the bags and took some of the food.

"Fill your water bottle from the rain bucket," Maggs mumbled from under the pillow. "Then wait for me; I'll be right there." In a moment, she was snoring again.

Outside, it was chilly and still quite dark in spite of the faint pink glow in the east. Lina filled her water bottle and put the food in her pack. She had no intention of waiting for Maggs. Already, she was too far to the south. To keep from getting lost on the way home, she needed to head back the way they'd come for a while and get to a spot that was familiar before turning toward Sparks. She could be well on her way before Maggs even woke up.

She waved at the sheep, who were huddled together in one big clump, and she stroked the side of Happy the horse, who swung his head around to look at her sadly. "Goodbye," she whispered, and she started up the slope, heading northeast, back toward Ember.

As she walked, she made a plan. There was that rock like a shoulder heaving out of the ground, she recalled. It was ten minutes' walk or so from the entrance to Ember, and it was near the stream. If she headed for that rock, then she could follow the stream and be sure she was going the right way home.

Wind blew her hair sideways, and she reached back to braid it as she walked, tying the end with a thread she pulled from the raveling hem of her shirt. Rest and food had given her energy, and she wanted to be going *fast*. She burned with impatience. But the long wet grass and soft ground slowed her steps, and she couldn't see very well in the dim light. She was sure it was just as early as it had been when she and Doon had started out from Sparks, maybe even earlier. She should get home, if nothing went wrong, before the end of the day. It wasn't soon enough; it meant a whole day and night of captivity for Doon. But it was the very best she could do. So she strode across the hillside as quickly as she could, munching on one of the carrots, with her damp pant legs slapping against her skin. The sun will be up soon, she told herself. Then I can go faster.

That same morning, just at sunrise in the village of Sparks, Kenny, Lizzie, and Torren met by the field at the far north end of town. The nighttime rain had stopped, and the first red rays of the sun shot over the mountain's rim, lighting the eastern side of each dry stalk of grass and clod of dirt in the field, and each fence post at the field's edge. It was cold, but no one minded. They had bundled up well, and they were excited by their mission: to rescue Lina and Doon and to have an adventure of their own.

It was a Saturday, so they didn't need excuses for skipping school, only for their families. Torren had told Mrs. Murdo and Doctor Hester that he had to go and talk to Doon about a very important matter, which was more or less true, and that he'd be back pretty soon. Lizzie and Kenny had both simply said they were going for a walk, and their parents let them go without questions.

The three of them went around the end of the field and started up the hill. Each wore a small backpack, in which they'd brought bottles of water and hunks of bread and dried fruit in case Lina and Doon were starving. Lizzie had also brought two extra scarves in case they were cold. Kenny, who had lain awake thinking about this venture most of the night, had stuffed his pockets with some scraps of cloth torn from an old red shirt. He planned to drop one of these every now and then as they walked and anchor it to the ground with a stone or a stick driven through it so that when they came back, they could follow the scraps and not get lost. He was a little worried about getting lost.

Lizzie had washed her hair the night before and then brushed it for a long time. Today, instead of braiding it, she had let it flow loose over her shoulders, which she knew made her look more beautiful. She had also rubbed her arms and neck with dried lavender, which made her smell good. She did these things because somewhere in the back of her mind was the notion that Doon, who always seemed to be doing something important, something other people admired him for, might want a girl companion who was a little more fascinating than Lina. If Doon was going to be a hero, he needed someone special by his side. Lizzie had always thought of herself as rather special. Even her illness hadn't diminished her good looks; in fact, she thought the thinness of her face and the hollows around her eyes made her look more interesting.

"I hope nothing terrible has happened to them," she said, panting slightly as they approached the crest of the hill. "What if they have frostbite? What if one of them has broken a leg or something?" She imagined Doon, limping on his mangled leg, putting his arm around her shoulders for support. No, first she would need to tie up the broken bone somehow with the extra scarf she'd brought. *I'm so grateful,* Doon would say. *It's a miracle that you were here.*

At the top of the hill, they stopped to get their breath and to look around. Behind them was their village. Wisps of smoke rose from chimneys, and a few people, breathing clouds of steam, hurried across yards or trudged down streets. The sun was just beginning to hit the east sides of the rooftops. A few windows flashed golden in the strong early light. From here, Sparks looked like a calm and contented village, not one harrowed by sickness and hunger.

"Pretty soon things will get better," said Kenny.

"Uh-huh," said Lizzie, who was imagining how it would be to come into town with Doon holding her arm and everyone seeing that she had saved him.

"Come on, let's go," said Torren. This was one of the few chances he'd had to be *away* from where he lived, and he wanted to make the most of it. Roamers didn't stand around looking back at the place they'd just left. They moved on.

Ahead stretched one line of hills after another, each ridge higher than the last, rolling toward the mountains in the distance. It was a vast and empty landscape, and when they contemplated it, each of the three travelers felt a shiver of doubt.

"Which way do we go?" Kenny asked Lizzie.

Lizzie wasn't sure, but she didn't want to say so. "It's sort of that way," she said, waving a hand out to the right. "After a while, you get to a stream, and then you just follow that."

"See those trees?" said Kenny. "The ones that look like a hand?" He pointed to a clump of oaks that grew in a sort of mitten shape near the top of a hill about three ridges away. "Let's aim for there. We can see a lot from that high, and I think it looks close enough so we can get home before dark."

So they set out, downhill this time, across fields of wet grass. Lizzie scanned the landscape for anything that looked familiar, but nothing did. At the same time, *everything* did, because it all looked the same. She was pretty sure they were going the right way, but still she was glad that Kenny set down his red rag markers every now and then, just in case.

All three of them slipped or stumbled sometimes, because they were not looking at the ground they walked on but were scanning the slopes all around, searching for any sign of Lina and Doon. But even after an hour of walking, when the sun had fully risen and their feet were already starting to hurt from rubbing against their shoes, they saw no sign of anything moving anywhere in the landscape except, far off in the distance, some birds with motionless wings floating in circles in the sky.

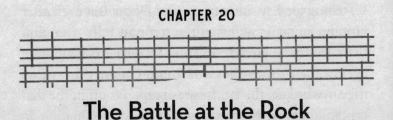

CHAPTER 20

The Battle at the Rock

Once he had rewrapped the diamond and put it back in his pack, Doon's first thought was of Lina. She couldn't have traveled during the night. There was a chance she might still be nearby, might just now be starting her journey to Sparks. How could he find out? He would have to get up high and look out over the hills to the west.

Even in the near-dark, it wasn't hard. He scrambled up the mountainside, finding roots and jutting rocks for handholds and footholds, until he came to a place flat enough to stand on. He turned around. The folds of the hills lay before him, receding into darkness. Was she out there? He filled his lungs with air and shouted. "Lina! Lina! Hello, hello, hello-o-o-o!" Would she hear him? Was she so far away that his voice might seem nothing more than the wind or the cry of an animal?

He waited, hearing no answer. Weariness overcame him; he might as well rest here a moment, he thought, before starting home. He sat down on the ledge with his back against the rock. His eyes closed—and when they opened again, the sky was lighter, though the sun was still behind the mountain.

He stood up and called again. "Lina! Are you out there? Lina! Hello-o-o-o-o!" And then he realized there was something else he could do. He slung his pack off, reached into it, and pulled out his generator. In a moment, his light was shining.

Doon's shouts flew out through the cold morning air and across the fields. Lina didn't hear the first one—she was still too far away. But she heard the second one. Though it came from a distance, she knew it was a human voice. Her heart jumped. Was it Doon? She had been walking now for half an hour and was within sight of the shoulder-shaped rock. She raced toward it, stumbling over clumps of wet grass. "Doon!" she called. "Is it you? Call again, call again!"

The voice rang out. "Hello, hello, hello-o-o-o!"

The Ember mountain loomed huge and dark against the sky, but toward its base she saw a dot of light—a bright, steady light that could only be one thing. "I'm here!" she yelled at the top of her lungs. "I'm coming!" But had he heard her? Could they find each other? With the wind at her back, she made her way to the great rock and climbed up its sloping side to the top. Here she shouted again and waved her arms. "Doon! Do-o-o-o-o-n! This way!" He's out of the city! she thought. We're all right now. We'll find each other and go home together.

She saw his light move, fade, and go out. He must have heard her, then. He'd put the light away and was coming. Lina waited on the rock. Little by little, the sky grew brighter at the edge of the mountain, though the mountain's shadow still darkened the fields. Every few minutes she called out, and she heard Doon's answering call grow closer. There was another sound, too. What was it? A sound of rustling, a sound of breathing. And then suddenly, right below her, a growl. She looked down to see three long, lithe, shadowy shapes in the grass. Animals. Their tails twitched; their heads were like spear points aimed in her direction.

Doon had heard Lina's answer to his call and with huge relief had made his way down the mountainside and started toward her. He put away his generator and strode as fast as he could out into the fields. He thought she must be near the big humped rock that thrust up from the ground near where the stream made a bend. For a while, they called back and forth. He guided himself by her voice, and soon he could see her, still small in the distance, standing on top of the rock and waving.

His spirit rose. He forgot for the moment how tired he was and hurried on, almost running. Behind him, the sky grew lighter. Lina wasn't calling anymore, probably because she could tell that he knew where she was. He went down the slope of a hill, losing sight of the rock for a moment, and veered slightly to the right and then up again, until the big rock looked hardly more than a five-minute walk away.

That was when he heard the scream. And with the scream came another sound—a sudden frenzy of barking. He stopped, baffled. Dogs? Why would there be— Then he remembered. Wolves were like dogs, Kenny had said. Wolves would bark.

His heart jolted, and he dashed forward. Another scream rang out, and Doon gave a shout in answer, too breathless and panicked to form words. He ran, stumbling, until he was close enough to see what was happening: Lina on top of the rock, and below her the wolves, stretching their long faces upward, growling and snapping their jaws.

Doon's knees went loose, but he willed himself to stay standing. He knew Lina had seen him. She was gazing at him with horrified eyes, too frozen with fear to call out. He was on a slight rise, perhaps fifty feet from the base of the rock, behind the wolves and a little above them. Their growling was terrible. It came from deep in their throats, a sound charged with threat and power. As he watched, one wolf darted forward from the rest. It rose on its hind legs, and suddenly it was immensely tall, its front feet reaching up the slope of the rock only a yard or so from Lina's shoes. Could wolves climb? Could they jump the distance up to Lina? Would they, at any moment, circle the rock and climb up the slope behind her?

Somehow he must scare these creatures away. He had no weapon but his own voice. He gathered his strength and gave a tremendous shout, packed with all his fear and horror. The wolves heard him and looked in his direction. Now he could see their faces clearly— the long, narrow mouths jagged with teeth, the slanting yellow eyes. He shouted again, and this time called, "Lina! Scream at them! Make noise! Throw rocks!" The word "noise" jogged his memory, and he reached down and yanked up a blade of grass. In a second, he had what Kenny called a wolf-scaring whistle. He blew, making a long ragged shriek. The wolves glowered at him, but they did not retreat.

Lina yelled, and the wolves turned back toward her. Without taking her eyes from them, she bent her knees and clawed at the rock beneath her, scratched away a handful of loose stones, and flung them down. For a moment, the wolves fell back, but only for a moment. Then all three animals leapt upward again, snarling and yelping, and Doon forgot his own safety and ran forward, yelling out terrible noises, flinging his arms about wildly. He stumbled, his foot twisted, and he felt a quick pain but ran on, hardly noticing. If only he had a weapon! Even a stick! But he had nothing, nothing, and Lina was in peril, and he was getting so close that any moment he would be among the wolves himself. If he could only somehow frighten them, scatter them—

He stopped short. His pack thumped against his back, and he ripped it off and reached in and pulled out the diamond. In one quick motion, he tore aside its yellow wrap. There was a split second when a needle of grief pierced him. Then he flung the diamond with all his might into the midst of the wolves.

But the diamond missed the wolves and struck the rock. It shattered into a million pieces, an explosion of glass splinters. The wolves yelped, ducked their heads, and staggered backward. Once again Doon yelled, and so did Lina, kicking down more stones. The wolves backed away, giving quick, violent shakes to their heads, still growling. Doon saw that their gray coats were thin and patchy. The stripes of their ribs showed on their sides, and on their faces and shoulders was the faintest sparkling where the light caught bits of the shattered diamond.

One of them seemed to make a decision. It trotted a short distance away and looked back, and the others, with a last glance at Lina, followed. They loped off, down the hillside to the north, and in a few moments they had vanished over the crest of a ridge.

Doon took in a long, trembling breath. He stood where he was, suddenly weak, as Lina climbed down from the rock and started toward him. "Are they gone?" she cried. "Are you all right?"

"Yes," said Doon, though he found he couldn't say it very loudly, and as soon as he took a step, a pain shot up his leg. His knees folded, and he crumpled to the ground.

Behind him, the sun at last rose above the mountain. Light flooded the sky, spilled out over the grassy hills, and glittered on the chips of glass that lay scattered over the ground below the rock. The remains of the diamond.

CHAPTER 21

Stranded

Lina ran to Doon and collapsed beside him. The energy of terror drained suddenly away, and she felt as if her whole self had turned to jelly. For a moment, she couldn't speak. She sat there in the wet grass, breathing in long shudders. Doon turned to her. "You aren't hurt, are you?"

She shook her head.

"Good," he said.

The wind blew against the side of Lina's face, and she shivered. "What was that you threw at them?" she asked.

"I'll tell you about it," Doon said, "in a minute."

Far up in the sky, big birds flew in circles without moving their wings. Lina remembered: they followed the wolves and picked over what was left. Go away, birds, she thought. There's nothing for you here.

"I'm going to go get my pack," she said after a while. "I left it on the ground behind the rock."

Doon just nodded.

Lina went, and as she came back, she saw Doon getting to his feet. But as soon as he stood up, he staggered and fell. She heard him give a grunt of pain.

"What's wrong?" she said when she came up to him.

"My ankle," he said. "I think I twisted it."

"Can you walk at all?"

"I don't know," he said. They stood up, and Doon held on to Lina's arm. At the very first step, he gasped when his foot touched the ground and yanked it up again. "It's not *too* bad," he said. "Maybe in a little while . . . maybe after I've rested some . . ."

"No," Lina said. "We can't make it back to Sparks by tonight; we mustn't even try. We'd have to go too slowly. Dark would come, and we'd be stranded out in the middle of nowhere."

Doon closed his eyes. He lay back on the ground with his face to the sun. It looked as if he was going to sleep. Lina jiggled his arm gently. "We need a plan," she said. "We have to get away from here. What if the wolves come back?"

Doon sighed and sat up again, propping himself on his hands.

"I know where we can go," Lina said. "Come on. Lean on me. Hop on your good leg."

Doon struggled to his feet and put his pack on. He

laid an arm around Lina's shoulders, and together they started across the hill, back the way they'd come. The wind came at them from behind now, blowing their hair into their faces, and the morning sun glared in their eyes.

Doon was silent the whole way, and Lina worried. Could he have broken his ankle bone? If he tried to walk on it, what would happen? But if he couldn't walk, then she was back where she started, having to go for help alone.

They headed uphill. It was a long, hard walk. Doon hopped and limped, and every several steps he had to pause just to give himself a rest from pain. They reached the cave entrance at last, but Lina turned away and led Doon through the thicket of trees to the room that Maggs had showed her. He would want to see it, she was sure.

"This is where the book was," she said. "That book you bought from the roamer. This is where they found it." The room was just the same as when Lina had seen it before—the smooth walls, the overturned table, the few dry leaves scattered across the floor.

Doon looked around. Lina had thought he'd be excited, but he seemed too tired even to be very interested.

She spread out her blanket, and they sat down. "Those wolves," Lina said. "They scared me right down to my bones."

"They were hungry," said Doon.

"Yes. I think I smelled like a sheep to them."

"You do have a sort of sheepy smell," Doon said. So Lina explained about Maggs—that she was the roamer who'd come to Sparks, and also the shepherd she'd stayed with last night, and also Trogg's sister, who'd been delivering food to his family.

"The lamb," said Doon. "We ate it last night." He told Lina about seeing her tricky note and how relieved he was to know that she was out safely.

"Did you eat any breakfast this morning?" Lina asked him.

"No," said Doon. "I've been up all night. A lot has happened. I have to tell you about it."

"Yes," said Lina. "We'll eat and talk." From her pack, she took the food Maggs had given her. "Here," she said, handing him some dry cheese and carrots and crackers. "It's kind of strange food, but it tastes all right."

So Doon and Lina ate, and he told her what had happened—how he'd got the key from Minny, how Scawgo had helped him escape, and how he'd cut Ember's power and trapped the Troggs in the Pipeworks.

Lina was worried by something in his voice—a sadness, a hopeless tone that wasn't like him. "Are you afraid Trogg might be coming after you?" she asked.

"He might," said Doon. "But if he does, I'll just tell him the truth: that I disconnected the generator so no more water will come from the pipes. And no more light from the lamps. He'll know he doesn't have a fortress to protect anymore."

"But wouldn't he be furious about that? And maybe try to punish you somehow?"

"He'd be furious, but I don't think he'd actually hurt me. Unless . . ." Doon trailed off. "We'll listen for voices or footsteps," he said, "and close the door of this room if we hear any."

For now, they left the door open. Day was brightening outside, and they could see the sunlight coming through the tree branches and hear the birds' first twittering.

"We'll stay here today and tonight," Lina said. "Tomorrow I'm sure your foot will be better, and we'll go home. Everything will be fine."

Doon nodded slightly, staring into the air.

"Really," said Lina. "It's all okay."

"There's something else I haven't told you," said Doon. "There was a diamond." He told her the story. "It was what we came here looking for," he said. "It's what the book was about."

"The jewel!" Lina said. "Maggs told me they found the book and the jewel together in this room. Nothing else was in here but those two things."

"And now the diamond is gone," Doon said. "It's what I threw at the wolves. I had such a strange feeling about it—that it was supposed to come to me. Maybe the reason was so I could use it to save you."

"That seems like a good reason to me," Lina said. "I'm going to go find some wood," she added. "We'll need to make a fire later on."

Kenny, Lizzie, and Torren had been walking for a long time now; the sun was past the noon position. Torren wasn't enjoying himself anymore. He hadn't done this much walking since the town hall burned down and he almost burned with it—would have, if it hadn't been for Doon. He'd scorched his feet in that fire, and even though they had healed now, a hike like this brought the soreness back. This wasn't turning out to be the thrilling adventure he had imagined.

"There wouldn't be any roamers out here," he said, "because there's nothing to collect and nobody to sell it to. It's boring."

"But roamers have to cross land like this," Kenny said. "This is what's between one place and another."

Torren frowned. "How much farther to those trees?"

At the moment, they were down in a valley between ridges of hills, so they couldn't see the clump of trees that was their destination. Maybe it was farther away than it had looked. It did seem to be taking a long time to get there.

"Well, we don't *have* to go all that way," said Kenny. He was a little tired himself. "We could just go to the top of this next hill. Probably we can see a long way from there."

No one objected to this. They climbed with renewed energy, and before long they came out on the wide, rounded crest of the hill, where the wind blew more strongly and the hills beyond looked steeper and rockier.

They gazed in all directions. Empty lands, everywhere.

"Should we eat some of the food we brought?" said Torren. "They aren't here, so we don't need to save it for them."

"We should eat it," Lizzie said. Her hair was tossing in the wind, getting all messed up and slapping at her face. "Or most of it, anyway. We ought to save a little, just in case they show up." She was very disappointed not to see Doon out in the distance, limping toward them, with Lina following helplessly behind, or maybe not with him at all. Sitting down to eat some lunch would be a good thing in two ways: it would give them a rest, and it would give them more time to see Doon and Lina if they really were out there.

So the three of them took the bread and dried fruit and water bottles from their backpacks, and then they put their packs on the ground and sat on them. They didn't talk much as they ate; it looked as if they had failed in their mission, and they were not feeling cheerful.

"You smell funny," Torren said to Lizzie.

"I do not!" Lizzie said. "Anyway, it's not a smell; it's a *scent*. It's *enticing*. But you wouldn't understand."

"You think you're so—"

But Kenny interrupted him. "Look!" he said, pointing. "Someone's out there!"

They jumped to their feet and squinted into the distance, against the sun. They all had the same thought: Our mission will be a success after all! But they soon saw that this wasn't a lone traveler but someone accompanied by animals and a wagon. The little caravan was moving south.

"It's not them," said Lizzie.

"Nope," said Kenny. "But maybe whoever it is has seen them."

"Let's shout!" cried Torren.

They yelled as loud as they could, jumped up and down, waved their arms. The traveler in the distance reached the crest of the hill where the clump of oaks grew that the rescuers had been aiming for themselves. Person, wagon, and animals seemed about to disappear down the other side.

"Louder!" screamed Torren, and they yelled with all their might. The faraway traveler paused, turned, paused again. Torren had an idea. "Lift me up!" he cried to Lizzie and Kenny. "Quick! Do a chair with your arms!" They did, and he leapt up, standing twice as high as his regular height, and waved and screamed some more.

And the traveler, followed by the caravan, turned and started in their direction.

"They're coming!" cried Torren. He jumped down.

"Hurry!" cried Kenny. "Let's go!"

They grabbed up their things and shouldered their packs. They ran, still waving their arms and shouting, and soon they were sure: the person had seen them, too, and was steering the wagon and animals toward them.

"I think it's a roamer!" cried Torren. "Isn't it?"

The person stalking toward them held a long stick and flailed it around, shouting. "Get going, flop ears! Over here, this way! Move those pointy little feet!"

"A shepherd," said Kenny. "A woman."

"Doesn't she look kind of familiar?" Lizzie said. "Wasn't she the one who came to town last week with the mangy sheep?"

"Yes," Kenny said. "I think you're right."

"Hey, there!" called the shepherd as she drew near. She and her wagon looked like a traveling junk pile, clanking and creaking. The sheep's legs were black with mud. The shepherd strode up to them and pointed her stick at them. "Who are you?" she said. "Why are there so many children wandering around out here?"

Kenny stepped forward and spoke up. "We're looking for our friends," he said, "who might be in trouble. One is Lina and one is Doon."

"Lina?" said the shepherd. "Long dark hair? Tall and skinny? Very quick in the way she moves?"

"Yes!" cried all three rescuers.

"She was up there by the mountain with the cave in it. On her way home," said the shepherd. "I'm surprised you haven't met up with her by now."

"But wasn't there a boy with her?" Lizzie asked. "Brown hair, dark eyebrows, serious-looking, handsome . . ."

"She was looking for a boy," said Maggs. "He was down in there."

"Down in where?" Kenny said.

"Down in that city in that cave." Maggs pressed her lips together and frowned, as if she might say more about this but chose not to.

"It was Doon!" cried Kenny.

"It has to be!" Torren said.

"We have to help him!" Lizzie cried. "We have to go and get him! Lina, too, of course."

"But it's late," Kenny pointed out. "It's too far to go; I'm sure it is. Dark would come before we got there."

"That's right, it would," said Maggs. Her sheep nudged up behind her, making mournful noises. She shook her stick at them. "Are you three from the town called Sparks?"

They said they were.

"If you're going to get home before dark, you'll have to hurry," said the shepherd. "You're off course. You've come too far south. You don't want to be out here at night. Go tell your people to get up there and rescue those two kids."

"We can't rescue them ourselves?" said Lizzie, disappointed.

"No," said the shepherd firmly.

"Then let's go," said Kenny. "As fast as we can."

So the three of them turned around and headed back to Sparks. The shepherd, with her scrawny horse, her rattling wagon, and her wayward sheep, turned southward again and trundled on.

CHAPTER 22

Return and Discovery

It was fully dark by the time Kenny, Torren, and Lizzie came staggering into the village, having walked at a breakneck pace for several hours. When they got to Doctor Hester's house, Torren ran up the path and flung open the door. "We're back!" he shouted. "Come here, everyone! We have to tell you something important!" Lizzie and Kenny crowded in behind him. It was warm in the house; the fire burned brightly. In a moment, Mrs. Murdo stepped out of the kitchen with a spoon in her hand, and when she saw them, she halted and gazed at them, puzzled.

"Torren," she said. "Where have you been all day?"

Poppy trotted out after her, but she barely looked at Torren and the rest. "I *want* some," she cried, tugging on Mrs. Murdo's shirttail. "I *want* some. I *want* some, right now."

Mrs. Murdo patted her absentmindedly. "In a moment," she said.

"We found out where they *are!*" yelled Torren.

"Who?" said Mrs. Murdo. "Hello, Kenny . . . and Lizzie . . ." She trailed off, sensing an odd level of excitement. "What are you talking about?"

"Lina and Doon!" cried Torren. "Someone has to go and rescue them!"

"Rescue them?" said Mrs. Murdo. "From what? Lina's down at the hotel."

Maddy came in the back door and gazed calmly at this gathering. She held a basket in one hand that looked to be full of weeds. "Hmm," she said. "What's going on?"

"I was the one who figured out where they went," said Lizzie, "after Kenny said they were gone."

"Gone?" said Mrs. Murdo, looking more and more confused.

"I want some *now,*" Poppy whined.

Torren jumped up and down in front of Mrs. Murdo. "The shepherd told us!" he shouted. "Lina's up there, and Doon is, too! They have to be rescued!"

At that point, Mrs. Murdo put her hands on her hips and looked stern. "All right," she said. "I'm missing something. Anyone want to explain?"

Poppy started to cry.

"What's the matter with Poppy?" Lizzie asked Mrs. Murdo.

"She's hungry," Mrs. Murdo said. "I've taken the last of the olive oil and was just frying a few potatoes, and she can't wait to have some."

"Maybe we could all have some," Lizzie said.

So they crowded in front of the fire, eating fried potatoes (there were just enough for three slices each), and Kenny and Lizzie and Torren told their story, all of them interrupting each other and talking in a great, urgent rush. Mrs. Murdo looked more and more horrified, and by the time they were finished, she was clutching the arms of her chair and glaring at them. "The town leaders need to know about this right away." She stood up and glared at Kenny and Torren and Lizzie. "You three," she said. "Come with me."

All that afternoon, Doon had slept and Lina had sat beside him, thoughts swirling through her mind of all that had happened in the short time—not even three whole days—since they'd set out on their trip. They'd left the door of the room partway open; light came in, and chilly air, and a few flying bugs, but no sound of animals or human beings. At about midday, Lina got out more of the food from Maggs, and they both ate. Then Doon slept again. Finally, the daylight began to wane, and the trees outside became a tangle of shadows. It grew colder, too, and Lina knew they'd have to prepare for the night: make the fire, eat the last of their food. She awoke Doon to look at his ankle and was shocked at how swollen and dark it was, like a big purple fruit. "I should be able to walk fine tomorrow," Doon said, but his voice was full of doubt. He sat up and leaned against the wall. "I can't stop thinking about the diamond," he said.

"But you don't know what it was," said Lina.

"No. But I looked underneath it, just for a second, when I came out of the cave, and I saw wires—it reminded me of when I used to take plugs apart in Ember to see how electricity worked. Wires were inside them."

"So maybe it was a light," said Lina. "But still—one light, I don't see why that would have made much difference to anything."

"Maybe not," said Doon. "But the strange thing is, it was here, right next to the way out of Ember, waiting for us. It was *meant* for us, just like . . ." He stopped.

Lina thought he was too upset to finish his sentence. But the look on his face changed. The sad, heavy look went away, and a look of surprise took its place. With his mouth hanging open and his eyebrows lifted up, Doon stayed speechless, as if suddenly turned to stone.

"What?" Lina finally said. "Just like what?"

"Just like the boat in the room," said Doon. "There was one boat, remember? And we thought, Why just one boat for all the people in the city?"

"Yes, and we were wrong, because really that was

just a sample, and once you found the secret door, there were lots of boats," Lina said. "But you had to know—"

"You had to know how to find them!" Doon cried.

"You mean there might be more?" Lina asked. "More diamonds?"

"There might!" cried Doon. "We have to try—" He struggled to stand up, moving so fast that he turned his injured ankle and said, "Yow!" very loudly and just barely managed to stay on his feet. "There was a steel panel in the boat room in Ember," he said. "And inside it a key. But I don't see anything like that here, do you?"

"No," said Lina. She lit a candle, because the light from outside was nearly gone, and walked with it around the edges of the room. The walls looked perfectly smooth to her. There was nowhere for a key to be hidden, and no keyhole to put it in.

"The instructions would have been in the book," said Doon, "if that shepherd hadn't burned up the pages. Let's try anyhow." He placed his hands on the wall behind him and ran them up, sideways, and down.

Lina jumped up. She stood the candle in a blob of its own melted wax in the middle of the room. "What are we looking for?"

"Anything that's different from the rest," Doon said. "A dent, a bump. I don't know."

They patted their hands over the entire rear wall of the room. If this was like the boat room, the rear wall was the one that should lead somewhere. Lina set up the table and stood on it to reach the high parts, and Doon did the low parts by scooching along on the floor. But every inch of the wall, as far as they could tell, felt the same: smooth and hard. So they moved on to the side walls. They pressed harder. Frustrated, they banged with their fists in a few places, thinking maybe they'd shake something loose. But the room stayed the same: no panels opened; no doors slid aside.

At last they set themselves to go over the wall where the entrance was. They were tired by now and losing hope, but they kept on, and after a while, Lina thought she felt a very slight seam in the wall. It was just to the left of the doorway. "This might be something," she said. "Feel it?"

Doon felt where she pointed. "Yes—just a hair of a crack. Try pressing beside it."

Lina pressed. Doon put his hand next to hers and they both pressed—and a small flat door sprang open, startling them both so much that they stumbled backward.

"Got it!" cried Doon, who had sat down hard on the floor. He struggled up, standing mostly on one foot. Lina was peering inside the opening, and Doon looked over her shoulder. What they saw was simply a handle, set vertically in the boxlike opening. To the left, the word "Off" was printed, and to the right, the word "On."

"Shall I do it?" said Lina. Doon nodded. She gripped the handle and pulled it to the right. It moved stiffly, but there was a satisfying click when it locked into place.

And then came a grinding, a creaking—and the walls began to move.

They jumped away and stared. On both sides of them, solid panels were sliding upward, revealing, all down the length of the room, shelves built within the walls from floor to ceiling, and on the shelves, lined up in neat rows, were blue diamonds exactly like the one that Doon had broken.

"Dozens of them," Lina breathed.

"Hundreds," said Doon. "They're so beautiful."

In the light of the single candle, the diamonds glimmered softly, blue as the evening sky before the stars come out.

"Our diamonds," whispered Doon. "The diamonds meant for the people of Ember." He gazed at them, his eyes gleaming. "Now," he said, "if only we knew what they were for."

CHAPTER 23

Home Alive

The three town leaders—Mary, Ben, and Wilmer—were not pleased to learn that Lina and Doon had gone out into the wilderness and needed to be rescued. At a time like this, Ben Barlow remarked sourly, wandering off on some crack-brained adventure and getting yourself kidnapped was a truly unhelpful thing to do. In fact, he said, it was almost criminal, in the circumstances, and when the two troublemakers were brought home, they should be given an appropriate punishment.

Nevertheless, everyone agreed that the children would have to be found. So Mary and Ben conferred with Mrs. Murdo about how it should be done. They decided to take one of the smaller, lighter of the town's wagons, one that could be drawn by a younger, speedier ox. Mary would drive the wagon. Doon's father insisted on going, even though Doctor Hester had told him the cut in his hand was infected and he'd have to have his bandage changed and the wound cleaned at least twice a day. Because of that, and in case Doon or Lina needed medical care, the doctor would of course go on the journey, too. At the last minute, Lizzie, to her delight, was asked to come along, because she was the person from Ember who had most recently been up in that direction. They would leave first thing in the morning, and they would take food and shelter and blankets with them, along with fire-making materials. Doctor Hester packed a bag of first-aid supplies: bandages, ointments, and splints.

When morning came, they set out, only Lizzie feeling the least bit cheerful.

The morning was cold but clear, and the ground less soft than it had been before, which made for easier travel. Lizzie stood in the wagon bed right behind Mary, who held the reins, and kept her informed about which way to go. "We went up on *this* side of the squash field," she said, "and then up the hill in that direction. Then when you get to the top of the hill, you'll probably see one of the red flags that Kenny put down. After that, you have to—"

"Thank you, Lizzie," Mary said. "No need to tell me the whole trip at once. Just say something now and then to keep us on the right track."

So Lizzie kept more or less quiet except for

absolutely necessary remarks, such as mentioning the first red flag when it appeared up ahead, or when she had to point out the mitten-shaped clump of trees that they had tried to make it to yesterday. She went back to the thoughts she'd had before, the pictures in her mind of how, when they found Doon, she would run to him and discover that he was hurt and be the one to know what to do, and he would realize how really special she was and—

The ox trudged on, and the wagon bumped along after it, over stony ground and clumps of grass, uphill and down, always heading northeast toward the mountains. The sun reached the midday point and began the descent into afternoon. Lizzie sat down in the back of the wagon. She brushed her hair (she'd brought her hairbrush with her, along with two spare ribbons and three scarves), and then, feeling sleepy, she rested her arms on her raised knees and put her head down on them. This was pleasant, because again she'd rubbed her wrists with lavender, and she was drifting off into a dreamy doze when Doon's father gave a sudden shout.

"Look!" he cried. "Someone's out there! Mary, stop the wagon for a moment!"

Lizzie jolted awake and leapt to her feet as the wagon slowed and halted. "Where?" she said.

Doon's father was standing, too, pointing north and east with his clublike bandaged hand. "Way out there," he said. "All I see is a dot, but it's moving—might be an animal, I guess, but I don't think so."

They all strained to see it. Whatever it was moved in fits and starts, slowly.

"Could it be a cow?" said Doctor Hester.

Mary shook her head. "Maybe a deer," she said, "or a coyote."

They stayed there, watching, for a few more minutes. Lizzie squinted hard at the moving dot, pressing her blowing hair to her head with both hands to keep it out of her eyes.

"Let's head toward it," said Mary. The ox heaved forward and the wagon wheels turned, and when they had traveled for another ten minutes or so, they were sure that the dot in the distance was not an animal. It was not a person, either—it was two people, walking close together, holding on to each other. Lizzie screamed, "It's them!" and Doon's father and Doctor Hester called "Doon!" and "Lina!" at the same time, and the two people, though they were still far away, must have realized who was coming, because each one flung an arm into the air and waved like mad.

Doon did have a wound, but Lizzie did not get to tend to it after all. Lina had already done that, and Doctor Hester said she'd done an excellent job. When they got back to Sparks late that night and the doctor undid the scarf that Lina had wrapped around Doon's leg and

Lizzie saw the blotchy purple swelling, she felt a little ill and was glad she hadn't had to deal with it just after it happened. She wasn't even jealous that Lina had been the one to save him. She'd sort of forgotten about all those rescuing visions as soon as she'd seen the two of them limping toward the wagon, weary and lame and smudged with dirt. They were both her friends, and she was glad they'd come home alive.

CHAPTER 24

The Salvage Expedition

That night, no one asked many questions of Lina and Doon, seeing how exhausted they were. But the next morning, the town leaders gathered at the doctor's house, along with Doon and his father, and they wanted information. Mary asked the question that was on everyone's mind: "Doon," she said, "you went into your old city, you say. Did you actually find useful things there? Food? Things we might use for trade?"

"Yes," said Doon. "There's enough to help us through the winter. I'm sure there is. And there's also—" He glanced at Lina, who met his eyes with an almost unnoticeable smile. "I mean, there's a lot. We have to go and bring things back."

"Why should we believe you?" Ben Barlow said. "You've caused a great deal of trouble already, and this jaunt out into the wilderness might just be more of the same."

Doon's father gave Ben a hard look. "Why *shouldn't* you believe him?" he said. "Has he not proved himself reliable in the past?"

"He has, Ben," said Mary. "I think we can trust what he says."

Wilmer pulled nervously at his ear. "Didn't you say people are living there?"

"Yes," said Doon. "But I think they'll be gone very soon."

"If we can bring back enough to ease our troubles," said Mary, "we should go."

So it was decided. Many people volunteered for the expedition, curious to see this underground city they'd heard about, and preparations commenced. Everyone pitched in. The candlemakers worked overtime, trucks and wagons were oiled and repaired, every spare sack and barrel and crate was found, tools and ropes and food supplies were gathered. The plan was to leave in a week, if the weather held.

On the second day of that week, after they'd spent a day sleeping and resting and eating, Doon and Lina met in an attic room in the Pioneer Hotel, a place that must once have been used for storing old furniture and cleaning supplies. It was a dusty, musty place, with cobwebs hanging from the rafters, but it had a window that looked out across the field in front of the hotel toward the river and let in a strong light they could see by. Their plan was to study, in secret, the diamond that Doon had brought back. They wanted to show it to no one until they knew what it was.

They discovered one thing right away. At the base of the diamond, within the circle of its gold collar, was a ridged hollow that looked like a socket for a light bulb, and indeed, when Doon found a bulb and screwed it in, it fit perfectly. But it didn't light up. He tried moving something near the socket that looked like a switch; but still nothing happened. Was this because the bulb was burned out? Or because the switch didn't work? Or what? But in any case, they could see that you could put in a light bulb, stand the diamond on its top, and if the bulb lit up, you'd have a kind of lamp.

They puzzled through the book of eight pages for clues. Lina sat on the floor by the window with the book on her lap, the dusty sunlight coming over her shoulder. Doon sat next to her with the diamond, which shimmered as the light hit it but stubbornly kept its secret.

"I don't see anything in the book that we haven't already gone over," Lina said. "There's just this, on the page at the end. It looks like it really is the last page of the book—I mean, there aren't any ripped edges after it. There's a half sentence at the top, I guess continued from the page before, which isn't there. It says, '. . . celestial source, perfectly pure, and for human purposes, infinite.'"

"What does 'celestial' mean, I wonder?" said Doon. "And 'infinite'?" He scrutinized the diamond's underside again, holding it up into the light so he could see. Besides the socket for the bulb and the switch, there were wires within the diamond's collar that looked as if they could be uncoiled. Carefully, he pulled them out, but he couldn't tell what he was supposed to do with them. He tucked them back in again.

He felt unbearably frustrated. This beautiful, strange object, which seemed to be a light, left by the Builders for the people of Ember—he held it in his hands but couldn't make it work. In Ember, lights worked by electricity, and electricity was right there in the walls of the houses. You put a plug into a socket, and the electricity came through. But this light had no plug, unless there was one that Trogg had lost, and even if there had been, there was nothing here in Sparks to plug it into. So how did the diamond get its power?

They found the answer a short time later. They didn't know at first *why* they'd found it—all they knew was that the light suddenly worked. But in the next few days, as they did one experiment after another and casually asked Ms. Buloware, the schoolteacher, for some word definitions, they began to understand. And once they understood, they made their plan.

* * *

During that week, Torren was in a state of unbearable excitement. Thrilling and mysterious things were going on all around him, and at last he was part of it, not left out. Or at least not completely left out. He'd helped to rescue Lina and Doon, and he would be going on the expedition. Sometimes, though, he had the feeling there were things he wasn't being told. Lina had the look of someone with a secret, a happy one: she hummed a lot, and often when Torren was talking to her, she didn't pay attention, as if she was thinking about something else.

Doon and his father came up to the doctor's house one day. While Doon's father was having his hand treated by the doctor, Doon and Lina went into a corner and talked together in whispery voices. Torren tried to lurk around nearby and overhear them, but Lina shooed him away. After that, Doon wanted to see Torren's treasures, so Torren got them out of the trunk where he kept them and lined them up—the airplane, the elephant, the remote, the box of light bulbs. "They're great," Doon said. He tapped the box of light bulbs. "How many are in here?"

"Forty-eight," said Torren proudly. "Well, no, forty-seven, because you took one for your generator."

"That's right," Doon said. "You're lucky to have them. Someday, they might come in handy."

At last the day of departure arrived. The morning

dawned chilly but clear. All those who would be making the trip gathered in the plaza. They swarmed around, toting empty bags and boxes to bring things back in, loading them onto four trucks, hitching up oxen, and all the time calling out to each other in loud or anxious or excited voices. Ben Barlow strode around making sure that the only people going were good walkers, since there wouldn't be room for anyone to ride on the trucks on the way back (except for Doon, because of his injured ankle). Mary Waters reminded people to follow the lead of those from Ember, who knew where they were going, and Wilmer Dent fussed with the buttons on his coat, looking nervous.

"Where's Doon?" Torren asked Lina.

"He's coming," she said, but she looked a little worried, scanning the crowd and not finding him, and very relieved, when at the last minute he came into the plaza, red in the face from hurrying, still limping a little, and carrying a bulky pack on his back.

Mary gave the order. "Let's go!" she cried, and with squeaks and rattles from the trucks and the bawling of the oxen, the caravan headed up the north road, around the far edge of the squash field, and up into the hills.

They traveled all day, and at nightfall they reached a sheltered valley where they made camp for the night. Another day of travel, and by the evening of the next day, they'd arrived at the cave entrance. The last of the sunlight came at a slant, throwing shadows eastward across the grass. The caravan halted, and everyone gathered around and stared at the arched opening in the wall of the mountainside. It didn't look very big or grand, not like the entrance to a city.

"That's where we came out of Ember," Doon shouted to them, standing up on the lead wagon. "And up around there"—he pointed to the right—"is where we go in."

But they'd need to spend another night in the open first and go down into the city in the morning. The trucks were lined up to make a barrier against the wind, and people scattered out across the hillside to break the low, dead branches from trees for their fires. Soon orange flames leapt in the darkness like waving hands.

Torren lay awake a long time that night. He was thinking that this was how it would be to be a roamer, except you'd be out here all alone in the wilderness and you'd have to make your own fire. And how would you sleep if you had to keep watch against wolves? It seemed hard. Maybe he'd decide to be something else.

Next morning, the wind was finally down and the air was a little warmer. Everyone rose early, eager to get started, just as the last stars were fading from the sky. But there were things to do before the descent into the city. People needed to eat, and they needed to get organized; and Lina and Doon had to put into action—or try to—the plan they'd kept secret from everyone. Now that they were here, about to make all this happen, Lina felt a fluttering in her stomach, and Doon realized that his heart was thumping a little faster.

While everyone was eating breakfast, Doon turned to Lina. "Let's go," he said quietly. He picked up his backpack, and he and Lina walked together behind the wagons and headed for the grove of trees.

CHAPTER 25

Light for the Journey

The door to the windowless room was just as they had left it—propped open about an inch with a stick. Inside, Doon set his backpack on the small table, which they'd stood upright when they were here before, and reached inside. He brought out a light bulb. "The reason I was late getting to the plaza the day we left," he said, "was that I had to wait 'til Torren was out of the house so I could go in and get these, and then I had to wrap them all up in Doctor Hester's rags and bandages so they wouldn't clink against each other in my pack and break. It took longer than I thought it would."

"But you got all of them?" Lina asked.

"I did. So here we go."

Once again, they opened the small door in the wall and moved the handle, and once again the panels slid upward and revealed the rows of diamonds.

"Now," said Doon. "We need to get one working." Gingerly, he lifted a diamond from the lowest shelf. He carried it outside, along with one of the light bulbs. Lina followed. They found a clearing among the trees, and Doon placed the diamond on the ground, in the full light of the sun, standing it upright on its collar of golden metal.

"Now we wait," Doon said.

They sat down on a fallen tree, side by side. They heard the voices of the people of Sparks in the distance, cheerful and excited. A bird hopped in the branches above their heads, making a tiny *pip-pip* sound, answered by another *pip-pip* farther off. A cloud of gnats danced in the sunlight.

The blue diamond sat there unchanged. They waited some more.

"Is it time?" Lina said at last.

"I think so."

They stood up. Doon picked up the diamond and turned it over. He screwed in a light bulb, flicked the switch, and the bulb lit up. It shone with the brilliance of a hundred candles, blasting their faces with light.

Then they ran, Doon carrying the diamond with its shining light bulb high above his head, back to where the people stood eating their breakfasts on the mountainside. "Look!" Doon shouted, and Lina shouted, too: "Look, everyone!"

People dropped their food and stared. Voices

rang out from everywhere. "What is it?" "Where did it come from?"

"Is it magic?" someone called.

"No, not magic," said Doon. "It's electricity!"

"Electricity?" yelled Torren. "Like with your generator?"

Everyone crowded around. They gawked at the shining light bulb—a miracle, its steady beam bright even in the morning sun.

"But I don't get it," Kenny said. "What makes it shine?"

"It makes electricity from sunlight," said Doon.

"No," said Ben Barlow, craning his head forward and frowning. "Impossible."

"And yet there it is," said Mary Waters.

Doon's father spoke up. "Son," he said, "you've brought this thing out of nowhere. How did you find it? How do you know about it? I think you need to explain."

So Doon and Lina explained together, telling the whole story—or almost the whole story. They left out the part about the wolves. Telling that, they knew, could only cause trouble. Mrs. Murdo would have nightmares about it. Doon's father would be aghast at the terrible risks they'd taken. The villagers might want to go after the wolves and kill them, though the wolves were only doing what all creatures do—trying to stay alive. So Lina and Doon did not mention those moments of terror and danger. They kept that part of the story to themselves, like a dark stone that was the secret partner of the bright jewel they'd brought back.

People wanted to touch the diamond and examine it. Hands reached out, shoulders bumped. Ben pushed through, saying, "Make way, please, I need to see this," and Wilmer Dent edged in sideways, and Lizzie said, "We had electricity in Ember; *everybody* had it."

But Doon backed away. "Wait!" he cried. "We have to get started! We don't have much time." From his bulging pack, he extracted the box of light bulbs that he'd "borrowed" from Torren.

Torren shrieked. "Those are mine!"

"Yes," said Doon, "and you'll be proud to know they're going to be used for something so important."

Lina and Doon climbed up onto one of the trucks. Raising their voices so everyone could hear, they took turns explaining what the scavengers should expect when they went down into Ember—the narrow path that led along the cave wall, the Unknown Regions, and the chasm. (They'd be laying a sturdier bridge across it with planks and pipes brought from Sparks.) "We'll know right away if people are still there," Doon said, "because we'll see their fire. But I think they've probably gone already." He explained that there would be search teams, each one led by former citizens of Ember. The teams would go to all the different neighborhoods, collect anything useful, and pile it in certain spots. The team led by Doon and his father would go down into the Pipeworks. Lina and Lizzie would lead a team to the storerooms. Clary Laine would lead a team to Ember's greenhouses, where she had been the manager, and Edward's team would check the library and the school. Other teams would cover the rest of the city.

The search would go on for about eight hours. Doon chose Martha Parton to keep track of the time by burning eight candles, one after another, in Harken Square. (Privately, he hoped that the Troggs might have left their hourglass behind, but he couldn't count on that.) At the end of eight hours, Martha would blow three blasts on a loud whistle. Then the teams would carry all they'd collected back through the Unknown Regions, put things into packs, carry them up to the top, and load them into the trucks to be taken back to Sparks.

It took nearly an hour to make the preparations. Doon gave each of the team leaders a diamond and a light bulb, and each person stood his or her diamond in the sun and waited while it soaked up light. (Doon had tested this, back in Sparks: in about fifteen minutes, a diamond could take in a charge that would last at least eight hours.) Meanwhile, Lina, who had brought along a ball of string, cut short lengths of it and passed them out to all those who would be leading the search teams. She also gave each person several sacks, which they'd use for collecting, as well as a few candles, just in case any of the light bulbs failed. (She and Doon had brought with them all the matches they'd saved from their trip.)

When enough time had gone by, people screwed in their light bulbs, flicked their switches, and jumped and yelped and laughed gleefully as the bulbs lit up. Maddy, who wasn't one for jumping and laughing, gave one of her rare smiles. "So," she said, "Caspar's ridiculous quest had one good result after all."

"Now tie one end of the string around the ring," Lina said, "and the other to your belt. That way you can carry the light and leave your hands free."

It worked pretty well, for a plan made up on the basis of so little knowledge. Doon and Lina led people the short distance up the slope to the crack in the mountainside. The two of them went in first, carrying only Doon's small generator. Once they were standing on the ledge, Doon stopped cranking, and they looked down. No light. Not even the faintest glow. "They've left," said Doon, and Lina said, "Good."

Then began the process of leading nearly a hundred people down the long, narrow path along the cave wall. Their diamond lights lit the way far better than candles, but still the going was hard, and many people were terrified. There were shrieks from those who tripped on a rock or stumbled too close to the path's edge and wails from those overcome by fear of the long descent into darkness. But at last the whole troop trudged out across the Unknown Regions, crept and tottered and screamed their way across the bridge over the chasm, and entered the city.

The stink of old smoke filled the air. The teams took a few minutes to organize themselves and recover from the ordeal of the descent, and then they spread out, moving through the streets to their assigned neighborhoods. For hour after hour, they poked into every room, hall, and stairway, every cupboard and cabinet, every nook and cranny, collecting what was useful and leaving what was not. It was a thorough search, but not a quick one. The former citizens of Ember were constantly seized by memories and often insisted on going blocks out of their way to visit the house they'd lived in or the place where they'd worked to pick up some small treasure they'd left behind; and the people of Sparks were so astonished by the city that they asked a million questions and sometimes just came to a halt and stared.

But as the hours went by, the search grew more businesslike. The conversations dwindled and the side trips ceased. At various corners throughout the city, piles of useful things grew higher and higher. Clary's team, out in the greenhouses, gathered seeds of several kinds of beets and greens and squashes unknown to the farmers of Sparks. Edward's team found, to his great distress, that the Ember library had been emptied out; but the three books in Miss Thorn's old schoolroom remained: the *Book of Letters,* the *Book of Numbers,* and the great *Book of the City of Ember.* No one could say that these were really *useful,* but they took them anyhow to remember the city by.

Doon's team, down in the Pipeworks, wound through the tunnels to the mayor's secret room, from which—as Doon had discovered—the mayor and his cronies had had no time to remove very much on that last, frantic day. Stacks of cans, boxes of light bulbs, and cartons of supplies still stood there, surrounding the mayor's armchair, his table, and his plate spotted with moldy bits of food. Doon remembered what Mrs. Murdo had said about seeing bulging bags on the walkway beside the river as the mayor was trying to escape. His team retrieved those, too. Just carrying all these things back through the tunnels and up the long, long Pipeworks stairway took that team all the hours of the search. Doon had thought there might be time for him to go back to his old home and look for his book of insect drawings; but at the end, he decided against it. The world above was so full of wonderful insects that he could simply start a new book. It would be far better than the old one.

Lina's team found very little in the storerooms. As the Emberites had known, the city's supplies had been nearly gone. A few rooms held forgotten boxes of safety pins and rolls of crusty string and tins of salt, and there were some cans of food—mostly spinach—

and some boxes of electrical cords and plugs. Lizzie found a stray pair of pink socks that she claimed for herself. Most of the other stuff was broken or spoiled and not worth taking.

But Doon had told Lina what Yorick said about the back room of the shop where someone had been hoarding. Lina was sure she knew which shop it was—she'd bought her colored pencils there. It was the shop run by the young man named Looper, who had been the mayor's crony in the theft from the storerooms. He'd also been Lizzie's boyfriend, and when she saw the piles of things he'd collected, she sputtered with indignation. "He told me he was taking just a *little*!" she said. "What a liar! How could I ever have liked him?" There were cans of food, boxes of paper and pencils (even colored pencils, Lina saw with delight), packets of soap, and still more light bulbs.

About halfway through the search, it was decided that some of the teams should stop searching and start toting things up to the surface. Doon's father, who wasn't able to carry things because of his hand, supervised this, sending some people to collect things from the various piles and bring them to the edge of the Unknown Regions, and other people to fill their packs and start up the path.

It was a very long day. Legs and backs grew weary; people had to take rests, sitting on the benches in Harken Square. Lina began checking back more and more often with Martha Parton, who was sitting on the steps of the Gathering Hall, keeping track of the time by burning candles. When only a few minutes remained before the search had to end, Lina left Lizzie in charge of her team and slipped away. First she ran across Harken Square, skirting the black rubble that was the remains of the Troggs' bonfire, to the house in Quillium Square where she and Poppy had lived with their grandmother, to see if she could find the drawings she had done then of the bright city of her imagination. She shone her light on the walls where she'd pinned them up—but they weren't there. In the bathroom cabinet, though, she found the almost-empty tube of the medicine called Anti-B. She put that in her pocket. Then she ran back to Harken Square and climbed the steps of the Gathering Hall. She went along the corridor, into the mayor's office, through the door that led to the stairs, and up the stairs to the roof. Once more, for the last time, she looked out.

The city looked as she had never seen it before, dotted with bright, moving lights, one here, one there, wherever the search teams were at work. Lights never used to move in Ember; the only light came from the giant floodlights fixed to buildings and the lamps in people's houses. Now all those were dark, and instead the lights of the searchers flitted like luminous insects along the streets and within the windows.

Martha's whistle blew—three long blasts. As Lina

watched, more and more bright dots emerged from buildings, moved along streets toward the collection piles, swarmed about for a bit, and then joined a stream of lights all moving in the same direction as people headed with their bounty out toward the meeting place at the edge of the Unknown Regions.

"Goodbye, Ember," Lina said. She said it out loud, as if the city could hear her. "Goodbye forever this time, my city."

Then she went down the stairs and out into the streets again to rejoin the expedition.

She found Doon standing beside the white rocking chair, guiding people into the line that led out toward the cliff. "We won't see Ember again," said Doon.

"No," Lina said. "But it's all right. I said goodbye."

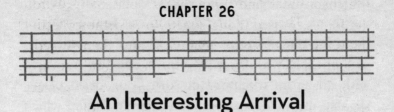

CHAPTER 26

An Interesting Arrival

The food from Ember was enough to get the people of Sparks through the last hard weeks of the winter. It made for a rather odd diet sometimes. No one in Sparks had ever eaten canned spinach or powdered milk or vitamin pills, but they were glad to have them, and glad to have the other things that had been scarce, like rubber boots and seeds for the spring. Everyone spent those weeks being a little bit hungry most of the time. But there were no conflicts, and no one starved.

Later on, when the ground had dried, several trucks went up again to bring the rest of the diamonds back to Sparks. It turned out that there were a thousand of them in the windowless room, stacked on long shelves in alcoves that stretched back into the mountain. Each household was given two, and the rest were carefully stored in the Ark, which now had a rebuilt roof. These would belong not to any one person but to the town, and the town as a whole would decide how to use them. Their very first decision was to use some of them for trade. A team went to the nearby settlement of Stonefield with three diamonds, and they returned with an entire truckload of corn flour, dried beans, slightly sprouted potatoes, and almond butter, which happened to be Stonefield's specialty.

The diamonds caused other changes in Sparks as well. They gave rise to a new routine, for one thing: every morning, even when the weather was cloudy, people put their diamonds outside to soak up sun; for an hour or so every day, the glitter of blue glass adorned gardens and fence rails and front steps. The candlemaker's business declined quite a bit; he had to branch out into making floor wax and wagon grease. Fewer fires started as a result of toppled candles, and people lit their way through the town easily at night, even in windy weather. The diamonds allowed people to work on tasks like knitting and sewing in the evenings—and to read.

Only a few weeks after the expedition to Ember, they had a real library to read in. Several people helped Edward build an extension onto the back of the Ark and line it with bookshelves, and Edward set up five tables in there, each one with a diamond in the middle providing light. Quite a number of people came in the evenings to browse among the books; even Kenny, who'd thought he didn't care for reading, found that he liked looking at one book in which there were pictures of astonishing animals—striped horses, spotted things with stretched necks, a giant piglike creature with a horn on its nose. Edward became known to the roamers in the area as someone who would buy books of almost any kind. After a roamer's visit, the library was sometimes actually crowded with people stopping in to see what was new.

Loris Harrow's injured hand continued to bother him for weeks. Finally, Doctor Hester decided there must still be bits of glass in the wound. She gave Loris some of her best pain medicine (which wasn't very good), and he clenched his teeth as she opened the wound again, this time under the bright light provided by two diamonds, and cleaned out the splinters once and for all.

One warm afternoon, when the last of winter had gone, a whole family of roamers came into town from the south. They were a wreck. Their truck was a rusty heap, with a filthy flapping canvas covering the back. They had one scrawny ox, one scrawny horse, and a flock of sheep that looked as if they'd been rolling around in the dirt. The roamers themselves looked as mangy as their sheep—matted hair, ragged dirty clothes.

Gradually, as the news of the roamers' arrival

spread through town, people gathered in the plaza to see them. A murmur of disappointment ran through the crowd when the sorry-looking troop appeared. The man who seemed to be their leader was a short, stocky person with wild hair springing from every part of him. He wore a pair of big square-rimmed glasses, though anyone could see that the frames were empty, because a few of his eyebrow bristles poked right through. He jumped up onto a stack of boxes and began his spiel in a loud, growly voice.

"Come and look!" he cried. "Bring your best goods, because you'll see that we have what you want! Unusual items! Things never seen before! Gather around!"

Doon had come into town that day to pick up some leftover scraps of lumber from the old town hall. Lina was at the bakery, buying bread. When the roamers came into the plaza and the man began to shout, both of them felt a jolt, as if they'd been suddenly struck by a flying stone, and they turned from their tasks and saw that they were right: the Troggs had come to Sparks.

Doon spotted Lina coming out of the bakery and waved urgently at her. She saw him right away and hurried toward him through the growing crowd.

"It's them, isn't it?" she said.

Doon nodded. The sight of the Troggs was doing strange things to his stomach and stirring up unpleasant thoughts in his mind.

"That woman is the roamer who sold you the book," said Lina. "That's Maggs, the shepherd, Trogg's sister. She looks even worse than before."

"And that thin, sad-looking boy with the twisted leg is Scawgo," said Doon. Seeing Scawgo struck him with a special pain. It was a complicated pain—sadness that he hadn't been able to rescue Scawgo, as well as gratitude for Scawgo's help. He hoped Scawgo had not had to take the blame for the diamond's disappearance.

"Step up!" Trogg shouted. "Look! I have canned corn and canned greens—it's from the ancient days and yet just as good as when it was cooked. I have thirty-seven pairs of eyeglasses! I have sweaters, I have mittens, I have shoes for babies. I have four bottles of cough medicine, only partly used."

People pressed a little closer. Lina whispered to Doon, "Are you going to say something to him?"

Doon's thoughts felt like moths fluttering in his head. What to do? Speak out against Trogg? Dash up and snatch Scawgo away?

"I have bags of wool," Trogg called. "Good for stuffing pillows, good for weaving. You'll need it for next winter, when that blasted cold weather comes again." He heaved three fat bags from the back of the truck and plunked them down.

"Nice, fluffy wool," said Maggs. "No burrs in it. No dirt."

"I don't believe *that*," Lina whispered.

"Also useful rainjackets." Maggs held up a garment that looked very much like the covering of her old wagon, patched together from crinkled old pieces of plastic. "I made them myself."

"Step right up," called Trogg, "and offer me some good trades for these exceptional wares. Especially welcome would be the fire-lighting gadgets I know you have in this town—matches. Special deals for those with matches."

People sighed and shrugged and shook their heads. They wouldn't get those special deals, because the town had no matches. They'd used the last one just a few weeks ago.

Doon felt a stab of a very unexpected emotion: he felt sorry for Trogg, who thought he knew everything. Trogg had had the key to light and power in his hands, but it did him no good, because he didn't know what it was.

The trading would start soon. Doon still wasn't sure exactly what he was going to do, but he knew he had to make himself known to the Troggs and to Scawgo. He had to speak up. He turned to Lina. "I'm going to . . . I'm going up there." He edged between the people in the crowd until he came to the front, and then he stood as tall as he could and called out, "Washton Trogg!"

Trogg jerked his head up. He spotted Doon instantly. His mouth opened as if he were going to speak, but there was a long pause before he did. Kanza and Yorick made noises of surprise in that pause, Minny wailed, and Scawgo cried out, "Doon!" in his high, wavery voice. But Trogg just glared for a long moment. Then his eyebrows came down like storm clouds, and his face crunched into a scowl. "Thief!" he shouted. "Sneaking, treacherous thief!"

The crowd of villagers went silent, except for a few people at the back, saying, "What? Why is he shouting? What's going on?"

"It's true," Doon said. "I stole from you."

"And after I was so good to you, taking you into my own family!" Trogg was purple with rage. He shook his hairy fist at Doon. "Traitor, ingrate, robber!" he screamed.

"Criminal!" yelled Yorick.

Trogg reached sideways and socked him on the shoulder. "Quiet!" He glared at Doon. "You stole from me," he said, "and you should pay."

"I *have* paid you," said Doon. "With my time. And my labor."

Kanza shouted out. "That's not enough! We were going to buy a castle with that thing!"

Minny let out a piercing wail.

Currents of excited talk ran through the crowd as people realized who these roamers were. The Emberites especially stared in fascination at the strange grubby people who had taken over their city. Lina, still standing at the back, heard them whispering to each other in tones of horror and outrage.

"My daughter is right!" shouted Trogg. "It's not enough!" He spread his arms wide and stared out at the villagers. "It's wrong to protect a thief!" he roared. "I demand justice!"

Before Doon could respond, another voice rang out. It was Scawgo, limping toward Trogg, then tugging at his sleeve. "It's my fault, not his! *I* stole the diamond. Don't blame him, please don't."

And that was when it occurred to Doon that he could make everything right—he could do it easily, right here and now. "No," he said. "I'm the one who wanted it, and I'm the one who took it away. So—I will give it back."

Trogg had been about to burst into another bout of rage. He had his fist in the air, ready to shake it at Doon. When he heard this, he stopped short. "What?"

"I will return what I took," said Doon. But he realized then that he couldn't—not right here, not this moment. He had no diamond with him. He stood there uncertainly, reluctant to walk away, not sure what to do next.

But Lina knew. "Doon!" she cried. "Wait one minute!" She elbowed her way through the crowd and darted into the nearest shop. In a moment, she was pressing through the crowd again, this time holding a diamond, and when she got to Doon, she gave it to him. He held it up so Trogg could see it. "Here it is!" Doon cried. "For you."

All the bluster went out of Trogg. He took the diamond and gaped at it, and his family gathered around him and stared, too. Minny stretched out a hand and stroked the diamond, as if it were a little animal. Kanza chuckled in glee.

Scawgo, though, was looking at Doon, and his face was sad.

The villagers watched all this, murmuring and muttering.

"Well," said Trogg finally. "You did the right and proper thing, Droon. Now that we have our property back, let's get on with the trading."

"All right," said Doon, "but first you have to listen to what I'm going to say."

Trogg shrugged. "Say it, then."

Everyone else listened, too, pressing up close. The mutterings and murmurings stopped.

"My name is not Droon; it's Doon. Doon Harrow. This town, Sparks, is where I live. And the city of Ember—which you called Darkhold—is where I was born and grew up. And so did about four hundred of the people who now live in this town."

"No," said Trogg. Kanza giggled nervously, and Yorick's jaw dropped open.

"Yes," said Doon, and a chorus of agreement rose from the Emberites in the crowd.

Trogg scratched his neck, frowning. "Now, hold on a minute here—" he said.

"No," said Doon. "You hold on." He told him about the people of Ember and how they'd left the city and come to Sparks. He told him how he and Lina Mayfleet had returned to the city and how their plan had been so horribly interrupted by Trogg and his family. "It's true," he said. "I took your diamond when Scawgo offered it to me. I knew it belonged out in the world, not with you."

Trogg made a noise of disgust. "Pfffft. How could you possibly know that?"

"I knew it because of the book you found with it," Doon said. "The book I bought from your sister. It said, 'For the people from Ember' on the cover. Besides," he added, "I was sure you didn't know what the diamond really was."

"I did, too." Trogg folded his arms and stuck his chin out stubbornly.

"What was it, then?" asked Doon.

"A *jewel*, nutbrain! I don't suppose you miserable, poverty-stricken people have ever come across enough jewels to know one when you see one."

"Maybe not," said Doon, "but I knew the diamond was more than a jewel." Trogg sputtered, but Doon held up a hand. "Never mind," he said. "Go on with your trading now. Pretty soon, you'll see."

Trogg scowled at him, but he put the diamond in

the front of his truck and then went back to his bags and boxes, and he and his family finished laying out their wares. Trogg held up each of his items in turn, and people called out their offers. The sun dropped lower in the sky; the shadow of the town hall and the shadows of the trees by the river lengthened across the plaza's stones. As the darkness deepened and Trogg carried on with his trading, Doon and Lina quietly walked all the way around the plaza, going into each shop and stall and speaking briefly with its owner. One by one, the shopkeepers came out of their shops, each with a diamond, its light bulb attached and lit. They stood in their doorways. Soon the whole plaza sparkled and glowed.

Trogg looked up. He ripped his glasses off, as if they might be interfering with his vision, and gazed into the brightness. He seemed utterly stunned. Doon went up to him and grinned. He couldn't resist. "It's called e-lec-tricity," he said. "Have you heard of it?"

CHAPTER 27

A Bright Future

After some long and heated conversations, the leaders and people of Sparks agreed to invite the Trogg family to become citizens of the town. There were many arguments against this: (1) the Troggs had treated Doon very badly; (2) they had treated Scawgo badly, too; and (3) they weren't especially pleasant people. But there were also a few arguments in their favor: (1) they could have been worse to Scawgo than they were; (2) Maggs had helped Lina; (3) Trogg was ingenious in some ways; and (4) they were clearly not doing at all well as roamers and needed help to become civilized people.

The Troggs were given an old four-car garage in back of the Pioneer to fix up for themselves. Doon taught them how to use their diamond, and Lina offered to teach them how to read. In time, they settled down fairly well. Maggs's flock grew healthier and increased, and eventually provided wool for many coats and blankets. Trogg invented a clever way to make collapsible shop awnings, and Yorick and Kanza learned that gloating, sniggering, pinching, and punching were not acceptable kinds of behavior and made some efforts to reform.

Lizzie changed her mind about becoming Doon's girlfriend. He was too serious, she decided, and besides, it was clear that he liked Lina best. Instead, she began trying to get to know Scawgo, the strange boy who had come with the Troggs. It was hard to get to know him, because he was very shy; but Lizzie was sure that someone as charming as herself could get through to him. She could tell that he needed laughter and encouragement and kindness.

Scawgo went back to his real name, which was Tim. He explained to Doon that the reason he hadn't ever tried to leave the Troggs was that he had no place else to go; he knew he couldn't make it in the world on his own. But now that he'd come to Sparks, he decided he'd like to live with someone else. He moved into the Pioneer Hotel with the Noam family, in a room on the first floor so he wouldn't have to climb stairs, and he made himself useful by helping in the kitchen. One day, he showed his treasures to Lina and Doon, the ones Doon had retrieved for him from the high shelf in the Troggs' apartment. There was a bracelet of glittery red stones that had been his mother's; a boar's tooth on a string that came from his father; three shiny pebbles he'd found in a stream; an ancient silver coin; and two things he'd found in Ember: a book full of beautiful hand-drawn pictures of insects and several drawings of a strange city that he'd discovered on the wall of one of the apartments he'd helped to loot. "My bug book!" cried Doon. "My city pictures!" cried Lina. When Scawgo found out that Doon and Lina had made these things, he offered to give them back. But Doon said he was planning to start a whole new bug book, and Lina said she'd like one or two of her pictures but that he could keep the rest. "I can always do more," she said. "There's endless drawings in my imagination."

Kenny sat on a log for a great part of the summer. He'd come across a fox's den up toward the woods, and if he was extremely quiet, the cubs would come out and play and he could watch them. Once he took Doon up to see them, too, and Doon told him about the fox that helped them when they came out of Ember.

The months following that hard winter were also hard, but in a different way. People were no longer struggling to survive. They were simply doing the hard but satisfying work of life: building, planting, cooking, sewing, trading, repairing, learning. Sometimes Doon complained to his father about working so much, when he was tired or when work hadn't been going well. His father had moments of weariness and discouragement, too; his right hand had never healed quite properly and still didn't work very well. But what he said to Doon was, "You know, son, I don't think there's such a thing as an easy life. There's always going to be hard work, and there will always be misfortunes we can't control lurking out at the edges—storms, sickness, wolves. But there *is* such a thing as a good life, and I think we have one here." Doon had to agree.

He spent hours working with the diamonds. He discovered a small lever within the metal collar; when he pressed it, a spark flashed up, startling him, and showing him that the diamond could be used like a match, to start a fire. He figured out how to unwind wires from within the diamonds' metal rings and connect them up to other things besides light bulbs. He found an old electric fan in a storage room at the Pioneer that he repaired, and when he hooked it to a diamond, the fan turned nicely, making a weak stream of cool air. He connected an ancient toaster to a diamond and burned up a few pieces of bread. He figured out how a diamond could run a water pump, if he'd only had the materials for making an electric pump in the first place, and how several diamonds could be hitched together to provide power enough for something larger, like a refrigerator, if ever a roamer should come through with an old refrigerator that could be made to work.

But mostly the diamonds simply showed what was possible: that the light from the sun could be caught and stored for the use of human beings. Understanding how this was done, finding the means of doing it, learning to make light bulbs, learning to make diamonds—these projects would take many, many years. Doon understood that they wouldn't happen in his lifetime. But he could begin. He could learn, he could make things, and he could teach others. He knew it was the work he would choose.

Lina made a discovery that involved something old and familiar and something very new. It happened because of a roamer who came through the town late in spring. It was Mrs. Murdo this time who was the first to see him. She was down by the Pioneer, taking some pickled plums to Maddy, and there he was coming up the road from the south, leading three horses. Two were thin, with saggy backs and drab coats, but one—dark brown, with a black mane—held its head high and had a lively step.

Mrs. Murdo was struck with an idea. It was such a good idea that she ran ahead of the roamer on her way back into the village, and she was breathing hard when she got to Mary Waters's house. "Mary," she said. "I think we could do something wonderful for Lina."

Mary agreed, and so it was done: one of the diamonds was traded for the brown horse, and the horse became Lina's. She named him Fleet and spent nearly every one of her few spare moments that summer learning to ride him. By fall, she could stay on even when he went at a gallop.

Time passed—more winters, not as dark or as hard as the first one, more wet springs, more hot summers. New houses rose; new fields were planted. Roamers came through with things the town needed, and sometimes these were bought with a diamond. In this way, little by little, diamonds ended up in other villages. The roamers told people in those villages where the diamonds had come from and what they were for, and in time light bulbs from the abandoned places, which had always been useless before, became items in the roamers' stocks. Sometimes people who'd bought the diamonds sent a message back to Sparks, asking to buy more diamonds or wanting to know more about what the diamonds could do. Doon wrote up a booklet of information in response to these requests, and the students in the school helped him make copies of it. In this way, the diamonds and the knowledge of them spread slowly up and down the countryside.

More and more, the villages in the area communicated with each other. The roamers, whose oxen walked slowly and who stopped often, were the main connection, so messages didn't go back and forth very quickly. This was what made Lina think once again about being a messenger. She began riding out across the empty lands to small settlements and towns, following the roamers' routes but going far faster than they did, carrying letters and small packages from one place to another. Sometimes Doon went with her, sitting behind her and holding on around her waist, out to the ruins of ancient towns, where he gathered up old electric shavers and hairdryers and plugs and wires that might help him with his work. Sometimes Torren went with her; he called it "going on roamer practice."

Lina taught Torren the song she'd heard from the old roamer about Ember. She had recalled the words by now, and she knew Maggs had had it wrong. Maggs had sung it this way: "What's hidden will come to light again, A diamond jewel more precious than gold." But those lines should have been, "What's hidden will come to light again. It's *far more precious* than diamonds and gold." The precious treasure was the people of Ember, just as Lina had understood when she first heard the song. The diamond was precious, too—but without people to find it, understand it, and use it, it wouldn't have had much value at all.

Most often, however, Lina went on her trips alone. Mrs. Murdo worried a little that she would have accidents, or meet up with bandits, or get lost. She's just a child, Mrs. Murdo fretted. And yet, she reminded herself, look at all the remarkable things she and Doon have done! It wasn't because they had extraordinary powers, really, but because of how well they used the ordinary powers everyone had: the power of courage, the power of kindness, the powers of curiosity and knowledge. Lina would be all right, Mrs. Murdo concluded. After all, she was growing up and would soon be deciding on her own what she wanted to do. She asked Lina to please not go out into the wilderness during the very hottest or coldest parts of the year, and Lina agreed.

Lina divided her time between helping Mrs. Murdo and Doctor Hester at home and going out on messenger trips. She loved embarking on these trips, readying the saddlebags Mrs. Murdo had helped her make, packing food and supplies, planning her route; and she loved arriving at her destinations and delivering the letters people had been waiting for. But most of all, she loved the trip itself. She loved slinging herself up onto Fleet's broad strong back in the early morning and setting out, first at a walk as they went through the village, and then, when they got out onto the empty roads, faster and faster 'til they sped forward at a gallop, and the rushing air flicked through Fleet's mane and made Lina's hair stream out behind her. Maybe there was no happily-ever-after, as in that book of Edward's, but there was happiness sometimes, and she had it now, doing what she knew she was born for—to carry messages and to go fast.

One day, on her way back from one of her messenger rides—it was nearly five years after the discovery of the diamonds—a bundle of letters slipped from one of her bags and fell to the ground. It was her fault; she hadn't packed very neatly. She saw it go, and she brought Fleet to a halt so she could get down and retrieve it. But one of the letters had somehow blown beneath his feet before he stopped, and it was torn to shreds. She picked up all the pieces she could find. It probably wasn't an urgent letter; it was for Edward Pocket, from a man in another town who was also interested in finding books. But it would be embarrassing to have to admit that she'd ruined it.

She stopped at the library to explain this to Edward. He wasn't there, but Doon was, bent over some thick volume with damp-warped pages. A thought struck Lina. She smiled to herself. "Doon, look," she said. She sat down beside him and spread out the bits of the torn letter. "I think most of it's here," she said. "Maybe you could help me put it back together."

"Sure," he said. He started moving the bits

around. "Let's see. This looks like it must say . . . and so then this would go here . . . and this . . ." He paused and looked up at her. "Haven't we done this before?"

Lina laughed. So did Doon. A look went between them, like a quick current of electricity.

Sparks grew and prospered in those years. New houses arose behind the Pioneer Hotel, built in clusters around small courtyards so families could live easily connected to each other. There came a day when one of these houses belonged to Lina and Doon. Poppy lived with them, and next door lived Mrs. Murdo, who created a neat and well-scrubbed place by herself until, a year or two later, she accepted an offer from Doon's father, who left his small cottage to be with her, and she did her best to tolerate the untidy but interesting heaps of small items he couldn't resist collecting.

Much, much later, on the site of the ruined city that Lina had seen from Caspar's wagon, a new city slowly began to rise, a city of bright buildings with glittering rooftops—not buildings so high they turned the streets into shadowy canyons, but buildings hardly taller than the trees that grew around them. It was a beautiful city, a sparkling, dazzling city, where trolleys powered by the sun carried people up and down the hills, gardens flourished in schoolyards and between shops, and ships with colored sails arrived at the harbor from distant ports. Lina never saw this city, of course—not with her actual eyes, though she had seen something very like it with the eyes of her imagination. But her great-great-granddaughter lived there, and she kept, tucked away in a carved wooden box, the fragile old drawings that Lina had done. She took them out every now and then to look at and marveled at how they caught the spirit of the city that Lina had never seen.

But all that was many years in the future. Now, in the warm summer after the expedition to Ember, Lina is out in a field of wildflowers with Fleet, Doon is trying to hook up an old hairdryer to a diamond, Mrs. Murdo is sweeping the courtyard of the doctor's house, and Doctor Hester is in the garden scattering corn for the chickens. Torren is sitting nearby on a tree stump with his airplane. He makes it swoop and zoom. He is trying to imagine himself in it, traveling off to distant lands, being the Greatest Roamer Who Ever Lived.

Of course, he can't get off the ground, and he never will. But imagine that he could. Imagine that he could fly upward, like a bird. He would see the green landscape of spring spread out below, with the river curving through it, the fields dotted with yellow mustard flowers and orange poppies, and the people out doing their work. Up higher, he would see beyond

Sparks, the roads leading to other villages and settlements, and on the roads the roamers who connect one place to another.

Then imagine he could fly even higher, like an airplane. Now he could see the vastness of the earth below. The mountains would look like crumpled cloth bleached white at the peaks, the lakes would glint like coins, roads would be threads, and the grassy hillsides and fields would be a green carpet as far as his eyes could see. Here and there, clusters of dots would appear where people had settled, but there would be wide distances between them. The world would seem beautiful and peaceful from up here; he wouldn't see the storms and quarrels and terrors that can make life hard.

And at last, imagine that he could fly higher still, as high as a rocket heading into space. From here, he would see the round edge of the planet. In the gulf between himself and the earth's surface, he might notice an object moving along on an unsteady orbit. Sometimes it remains so high above the earth that a person below could mistake it for a slow-moving meteor or comet; sometimes it swoops very close to the earth. It is what many people in the area had noticed lately—most of them thought it was a traveling star. But it isn't a star at all. It's a small unmanned spacecraft that set out toward Earth more than two hundred years ago, after an astronomer named Hoyt McCoy, who lived in a town called Yonwood, made the first contact between the human race and beings on another world.

At the time, his discovery was kept secret except for a privileged few. Other scientists were told and so was the president of the country, who paused for a moment in his rush to war to contemplate what this discovery might mean. Eventually, some years later, the news leaked out. Newspapers ran headlines about little green men, and people got very excited. But after a while, when no little green men showed up, the usual concerns of life took over again, and the small craft making its way through space was nearly forgotten. Fifty years passed. Then came the great Disaster—and after that, there was no one who remembered it at all.

But the spacecraft continued its journey, and those who had sent it continued to monitor its progress over the many decades of its flight. Finally, a few months before Lina and Doon made their trip back to Ember, it arrived. It has been collecting data to send back to its home planet. It will report that the magnificent and powerful civilization it had expected to find seems to have disappeared and that a much smaller and humbler one has taken its place. It will observe that a great part of this world lies in darkness during the night, but not all. In some places, sparks of light shine—not fires but electric lights, bright gleaming spots like diamonds in the darkness. The people here seem not to have lost *everything* that came before, the little craft will report. Some of them have survived; some of their learning has, too. It seems clear that they are making a new start.

WHY DID THE BUILDERS CREATE EMBER?
WHAT WAS THE WORLD LIKE
BEFORE THE DISASTER?

Don't miss the exciting prequel to
The City of Ember!
Turn the page for a peek at ...

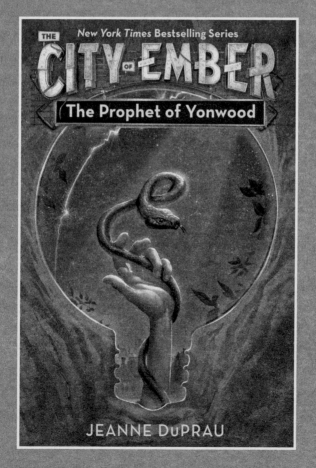

Nickie had actually never been to her great-grandfather's house in Yonwood, except for one time when she was too young to remember. But she'd made up a picture of Yonwood in her mind that she was sure must be close to the truth: it was rather like a Swiss ski village, she decided, where in the winter there would be log fires in fireplaces and big puffy comforters on the beds, and the snow would be pure white, not filthy and gray as it was in the city. In summer, Yonwood would be warm and green, with butterflies. In Yonwood, she would be happy and safe. She desperately wanted to go there.

After days of arguing, she finally convinced her mother to let her at least see the house before it was sold. All right, her mother said. Nickie could take a couple of weeks off school, drive down with Crystal (her mother couldn't leave work), and help her get the place fixed up and put on the market. Nickie agreed, but her real plan was different: somehow she would persuade Crystal to keep the house, not sell it, and she and her mother (and her father, when he came back) would go and live there, and everything would be different, and better.

That was her Goal #1. But since she was sure this was going to be a life-changing trip, she thought she might as well add other goals as well. Altogether, she had set herself three:

1. To keep her great-grandfather's house from being sold so she could live in it with her parents.
2. To fall in love. She was eleven now, and she thought it was time for this. Not to fall in love in a permanent way, just to have the experience of being madly, passionately in love. She knew she was a passionate person. She had a big love inside her, and she needed to give it.
3. To do something helpful for the world. What that would be she had no idea, but the world needed help badly. She would keep her eyes open for an opportunity.

They were driving now up the town's main business street. It was in fact called Main Street—Nickie saw the name on a sign. They passed the church whose steeple Nickie had seen from the highway. In front of it was a two-legged wooden sign that said, in hand-painted letters, "Church of the Fiery Vision." Nickie could tell, though, that the sign used to say something else; the old name of the church had been painted over.

Beyond the church, the shopping district began.

Probably it was pretty in summer, Nickie thought, but now, in February, it had a gray and shuttered look, as if the buildings themselves were cold. Some stores were open, and people walked in and out of them, but others looked permanently closed, their windows dark. There was a movie theater, but its ticket booth was boarded up. There was a park, but its swings and picnic tables were wet and empty.

Crystal turned left, drove uphill for a block, and turned right on a street lined with old houses. On one side of this street—it was Cloud Street, its sign said—the ground sloped upward, so that the houses stood up high, at the crest of their lawns. They were huge houses, with columns and wide porches and numerous chimneys. The people in there, Nickie thought, would be sitting beside roaring fires on an evening like this, probably drinking hot chocolate.

"It's this one," said Crystal, drawing in toward the curb.

Nickie gasped. "*This* one?"

"I'm afraid so." Her aunt stopped the car, and Nickie gaped at the house, stunned. Rain poured down, but she opened the window anyway, to get a better look.

It was more of a castle than a house. It loomed over them, immense and massive, three stories high. At one corner was a tower—round, with high windows. The steep slate roof bristled with chimneys. Rain ran down it in sheets, glistening in the last of the daylight.

"You *can't* sell this house," Nickie said. "It's too wonderful."

"It's awful," said her aunt. "You'll see."

A gust of wind dipped the branches of a pine tree that grew close to the house, and Nickie thought she saw a light in a high window.

"Does anyone still live here?" she asked.

"No," said Crystal. "Just the mice and cockroaches."

When Nickie looked up again, the light was gone.

YEARLING

Turning children into readers for more than fifty years.

Classic and award-winning literature for every shelf.
How many have you checked out?

**Find the perfect book, play games,
and meet favorite authors at RandomHouseKids.com!**